Then, as if someone had whispered them a special request, the band struck the opening bars to a familiar song.

In Alessandro's embrace, breathing in his scent, Rose was already reminiscing about Athens. When the music began, she was transported back there. "Songs, smells—they are like a time machine, aren't they?"

"Do you ever think about Athens?" he asked.

In the past week, she'd done nothing else. Their walks, their conversations, leaning toward one another over small candlelit tables. And also this.

Dancing. Bodies pressed together. Swaying. Moving against each other. Sharing the same air. The same breath.

His embrace tightened and she longed to lean into it. Surrender to it.

But no, there was no point. That would only make the next few weeks harder.

"I remember," he prompted, whispering into her ear, his breath sliding down her neck like a kiss.

The silent agreement they had to n~~ot~~ past was now close to ~~b~~ into dust.

Dear Reader,

If I hadn't been a lawyer or a writer, I would love to have been an archaeologist. Writing about Rose, an archaeologist in search of ancient treasure, has allowed me to indulge this side of myself. Rose has had her share of heartache and finds comfort in history, mysteries and stories from the past.

Rose's other half, the lovely Alessandro, is perfect for her. Except that he abandoned her unexpectedly a decade and a half ago. And now he wants to build a hotel on the same land she's going to excavate. Just like he was fifteen years ago, Alessandro is divided between his loyalty to his family and his love for Rose.

But Rose is about to find out that Alessandro may have had a good reason for leaving her and that her feelings for Alessandro may not be buried in the past, as she once thought.

Thank you for reading Rose and Alessandro's story. I hope you enjoy it as much as I loved writing it.

Justine xx

Back in the Greek Tycoon's World

—

Justine Lewis

Recycling programs for this product may not exist in your area.

ISBN-13: 978-1-335-59633-8

Back in the Greek Tycoon's World

Harlequin Enterprises ULC
22 Adelaide St. West, 41st Floor
Toronto, Ontario M5H 4E3, Canada
www.Harlequin.com

Printed in U.S.A.

Justine Lewis writes uplifting, heartwarming contemporary romances. She lives in Australia with her hero husband, two teenagers and outgoing puppy. When she isn't writing, she loves to walk her dog in the bush near her house, attempt to keep her garden alive and search for the perfect frock. She loves hearing from readers, and you can visit her at justinelewis.com.

Books by Justine Lewis

Harlequin Romance

Billionaire's Snowbound Marriage Reunion
Fiji Escape with Her Boss

Visit the Author Profile page
at Harlequin.com.

For my brainstorming and coffee buddy, Samara.
To many more afternoons in a booth at Tilley's xx.

CHAPTER ONE

THERE ARE SOME things one just can't capture on camera, even a high-end DSLR, and the view from the point over the Ionian Sea was one of them. Oh, one could capture the sun sparkling on the azure water, the light bouncing off the white rooftops and even the magnificence of the almost vertical white cliffs that dropped suddenly down to the sea. But one couldn't capture the smell of salt on the breeze or the way the sun warmed the skin.

The camera also couldn't capture the way Rose's heart swelled to be back in Greece, or the anticipation she felt at what she might finally find on this dig. She'd lived a nomadic life since she was a teenager, but Greece kept calling her back—more than Italy, or Sicily, or Turkey. Certainly more than her native Birmingham with its low, grey skies.

It was her passion for Greece—or, to be more accurate, ancient Greece—that had led her to her career in archaeology. One night when she was seven, she'd picked up a book of Greek myths she'd got from school. She'd read it in bed each night as her parents had fought and then, when her father had left, she'd read every other book about ancient Greece she'd been able to find at her school library. Then everything she'd been able to find at the public library.

Ancient Greece was the land of myths, monsters and legends, where history and fiction were almost as one—the land of Trojan Horses, labyrinths, gods and goddesses. Most importantly, a place where a man might be away from his family for twenty years and still return home.

Unlike her own father. She hadn't seen him since the night he'd left Rose and her mother to have a second family with a woman he'd met on a work trip. A year later, Rose and her father had shared their very last conversation. 'It's best if we don't see one another any more. We have different lives now,' her father had said.

'He has a new family—he doesn't need us,' her mother had said, as Rose had lain on her bed and bawled.

Rose had been replaced. She'd not been enough.

She exhaled, wiped the sweat from her brow and put her hat back on. It was good to be back in Greece and finally have the chance to excavate on Paxos. She had never had the opportunity to work on the Ionian Islands, the special, sometimes overlooked, western side of Greece that also had a shared history with the Italians.

The Ionian Sea had been the birthplace of Odysseus, the hero of Homer's *Odyssey*, who returned home to Ithaca after twenty years away. While her colleagues generally believed Homer's poems were entirely fictional, a series of discoveries over the past decade had suggested there were Bronze Age ruins yet to be discovered on these islands.

Recently, a three-thousand-year-old royal palace had been found just over the sea on Ithaca. More Bronze Age ruins had been found nearby on the mainland at Pylos. It remained to be seen whether any of these finds could categorically be linked to Odysseus and Homer's verse, but Rose wanted to be there if they were.

A team from the Athens Museum had been asked to conduct a survey of this particular site on Paxos. A hotel had been planned for it; however, a routine survey for the building permit had revealed some unusual things in the ground. Her old mentor in Athens had called her immediately, knowing her special interest in the Ionian islands. Not only would she have the opportunity to dig at someone else's expense, but they wanted her to lead the excavation. It was the first major dig she'd been asked to lead and a remarkable opportunity to be entrusted with. If she did a good job, she'd earn tenure for life.

She'd left London as soon as she could. A week later, she was on Paxos. She was staying in a small village called Ninos, standing in the late summer sun and hoping that what the surveyors had noticed in the ground would turn out to be something amazing.

The area they were digging was about half the size of a football field. Up the hill from them was an existing hotel. Down the hill were some olive trees and a path that led down to some more houses. To her right, the earth dropped away to the magnificent Ionian Sea. As workplaces went, it didn't get much better than this.

Rose stood for a much-needed stretch and walked over to the bag containing her water bottle. She drank from it gratefully and studied the height of the sun. It was early afternoon; they still had quite a few hours left in the day.

A silhouette on the hill made her heart hit her throat with a surprising thud. There was something so familiar about it...

It couldn't be him.

The man was pacing along the fence line that divided the old hotel from the land for the new one. He was definitely watching the team. His shoulders were tense and his gait rigid, but she couldn't make out his face with the sun behind him.

It's just the smell of the Greek air playing tricks on you. It'd be too much of a coincidence.

The last time she'd seen Alessandro he'd climbed out of her warm bed, slipped on a pair of chino shorts, pressed his lips to hers and told her he'd see her that night in the taverna down the lane. She'd worn her new white linen dress, an extravagance she'd barely been able to afford on her meagre student income, and had waited for him—for three hours! She'd felt worried at first, then foolish. Finally, she had returned to his room in the university dormitory, found it empty and had been furious.

He hadn't just stood her up; he'd cleared out his dorm room and left Athens. That ruled out him having been involved in a horrible accident or somehow having been detained and left only ghosting. It was bad enough that he had broken up with her, after all they had shared over the previous few weeks. Instead he'd made her wait for three hours, all dressed up and alone in the taverna, while he'd packed up his things and left without a word.

She'd called and called for days but he hadn't picked up. Finally, nearly a week later, he'd called her. It had been the strangest, most heart-breaking conversation of her life. Even more awkward than the handful of conversations she'd had with her father after he'd left.

'I'm sorry, I had to leave. I can't see you any more.'

'You said you loved me.'

He hadn't responded and her plea had felt pitiful. 'Our lives are on different paths now and it's best if we don't contact one another.'

He'd sounded exactly like her father.

And, just like her father, Alessandro had found someone else. Or, rather, he'd already been seeing someone else when he'd met Rose. Despite knowing that she ought not to try and find out what Alessandro's excuse was, a few months later she had searched for him and seen the photos. Alessandro had been holding the hand of one toddler and had another in his arms. The caption had been in Greek, but she'd made out the words *Alessandro Andino and his new twins* before she'd shut her laptop. She hadn't needed to know more.

Rose lowered her head, made sure her hat covered her face and went back to work. Whoever this man watching them was, he was no concern of hers. They were still at the stage of using small trowels to systematically remove the earth from the site. But with each trowel's worth she felt herself uncovering older, more ancient ground.

Snatches of other ancient memories came back to her. Alessandro had told her he had grown up in the Ionian, near Corfu, but had never told her where. Corfu was not far to the north, so maybe Paxos was the place. He hadn't told her much about his family; his mother had died when he'd been a baby and his father when he'd been a teenager. He had an older brother, she recalled. He hadn't spoken much about where he'd grown up, except to tell her he had no intention of ever living back on the islands.

He and Rose had been going to work their way around the world together... She scoffed. Everything he'd told her had been a lie.

Rose looked out carefully from under her hat. The man had begun his descent down the hill and had moved out of the path of the sun. As his face came into focus, her stomach began to drop. Thirteen years? Or was it fourteen? He bore an uncanny resemblance to the man she'd fallen in love with all those years ago.

The man approached Gabriel, her second in charge, and his deep, resonant voice drifted to her on the sea breeze and she knew.

Her chest felt tight and she dropped her head. *Nothing* he'd told her had been the truth. Not his plan to be a journalist, not his desire to travel the world and certainly not the passion he'd felt for her.

Foolish...that was what she was. The connection they'd shared had been so intense, so close that at times it had felt as though they could read one another's minds. But that too, had been a lie, just a trick.

Now she was older, she understood his game better than she had as a naive twenty-year-old: seduce the undergrad exchange student, sleep with her for a few weeks and lie to her about having a family. Get her to share her dreams, thoughts and desires, but reveal nothing about his actual life. Rose knew that he'd loved Shakespeare and had wanted to change the world, but she hadn't known exactly where he'd grown up. Or that he had children.

To be fair to her twenty-year-old self, she'd also thought she'd have more time to ask the mundane questions. She'd thought she'd see him again. She'd trusted him.

She'd never made that mistake again.

And she wasn't about to start now.

She had to brace herself: they were coming towards her. What on earth was he doing here? Writing a story on the dig? Perhaps, but he was dressed reasonably formally, wearing trousers and a collared shirt, albeit no tie. She'd answer some questions for him, tell him the excavation was just a formality, make the dig sound less exciting than she thought it was and he'd be on his way. No way was he getting the scoop about what she hoped would be the greatest find in the Ionian Sea in decades.

Once upon a time she'd had a short speech prepared in case she ever ran into him again. Even if she could remember that speech now, it was far from suitable to deliver it with half a dozen colleagues listening in.

'Rose.' Gabriel called her name and she had no

choice but to stand, push back her hat and summon every ounce of her dignity.

Dignity was hard to come by when she met his eyes, as dark and deep as ever, with dark hair and olive skin to match—because he was, of course, your archetypal Adonis. His classic Mediterranean looks had drawn her to him in the first place: a pair of chiselled cheekbones, a perfectly defined jaw, eyelashes so thick they almost obscured his eyes, especially when his lids were half-closed when he was… She took a deep breath and shook away the memory.

'Rose, this is Alessandro Andino.' Gabriel introduced her. 'Mr Andino, Dr Taylor is leading the excavation.'

'Mr Andino.' Her mind left her body as she said his name for the first time in years.

'Dr Taylor,' he replied, and his voice vibrated in her chest. Neither of them added, 'Pleased to meet you.'

Alessandro held out a large hand and she stared at it, her body unwittingly recoiling. She couldn't touch him. Her heart was beating fast enough as it was. Physical contact might just bring back too many memories of summer nights in Athens and tip her over the edge of whatever precipice she was standing on.

She held up her dirt-covered hands. 'I'm sorry, you don't want to touch my dirty hands.'

A glint flickered across his dark eyes but was

gone before she could make out its meaning. He placed his own hands behind his back.

'Rose, Mr Andino manages the Aster chain of hotels. He is the one who wishes to build on this site.'

He was a hotel developer—Alessandro Andino? The man who had once spent a whole night reciting Shakespeare's sonnets to her? Whose heroes were Jane Goodall and Rachel Carson? The same Alessandro who had been a term away from finishing his Master's in International Relations? That same Alessandro was a hotel developer?

He really had changed since they'd known one another.

Stupid. Everything he ever told you was a lie. None of it was ever true.

Alessandro shifted from foot to foot. His long-held plans were unravelling before his eyes. When the people from the Athens Museum had arrived two weeks ago, they'd told him it would only take a week at most to investigate the land and certify it as free for development. As far as he was concerned, the survey had only been a legal formality. The area around the village did not have any other known ruins, and besides, this was the Ionian Sea: most of the significant ancient finds were to the east, in the Aegean.

The Ionian Sea, for all its beauty, had not been the epicentre of ancient Greek civilisation. There were myths about everywhere in Greece, but that was all they were—stories. There was no reason to believe that the land they had purchased next to his hotel hid anything of real historical significance.

But today the team of two had tripled. That was good, he told himself; it meant they would finish sooner rather than later. But his gut had niggled with doubt. And the doubt had grown to full-blown worry when he'd looked down at the excavation and seen the woman. She was new, wearing a large sun hat and white shirt, gesturing to the others.

She was too far away for him to make out her face, or hear exactly what she was saying, but he could tell by their body language that the others were all deferring to her.

Deciding he should meet the person leading the survey sooner rather than later, he'd headed down the hill towards the dig. As he'd approached an English accent had reached him through the air and something inside him had twisted. He'd always been a sucker for an English woman, but had learned to give them a wide berth—for everyone's sake.

He looked at the woman again.

What were the chances?

He'd never been a lucky person; his life had been blessed with what one would call more sadness and duty than luck. But did the gods loathe him so much they would send her here? Now?

He studied her as well as he could without looking directly at her. As if he was trying to study the sun without burning his retina.

A man approached Alessandro and introduced himself as Gabriel, an archaeologist.

'You'll have to meet Rose—I mean, Dr Taylor. She's in charge of the excavation.' When the other man had said her name, Alessandro's heart had plummeted to his knees.

Dr Taylor. The shock he felt at seeing her was mixed with another feeling—pride. The ambitious, passionate student he'd known was now in charge of a survey. Or excavation.

Before he could digest whether this change in term would be significant, Gabriel was leading him over to Rose, who pushed herself up from her kneeling position to meet him. She brushed herself down and adjusted her hat.

She's nervous.

She shouldn't be nervous. He was the one who should expect recriminations; after all, he was the one who'd abandoned her.

You did it to protect her.

Rose's heart had belonged to her work. She would not want to have lived her life on a tiny island helping him take care of two infants.

Gabriel took him to Rose so quickly he didn't have time to prepare his heart rate, much less come up with some sort of explanation for having left her that day in Athens. And, once she took off her hat and he saw her face properly, her beautiful red hair in a messy bun with tendrils escaping around her face, he was completely lost. His head was only full of heat, her soft skin against his and the taste of summer nights.

He made it through the introductions in a daze but, when he offered her his hand and she refused, he was jolted back to reality. Oh, her hands might have been dirty, but she made it very clear she didn't want to touch him. His mouth went dry and he swallowed to get the next words out.

'Dr Taylor,' he repeated, like a fool.

She hadn't acknowledged knowing him, so he wouldn't either. This might be his land, but it was still her workplace. And she was in charge.

At any other time, he'd be delighted for her—running her own projects had been her dream. Right now, it meant she was the one he had to speak to, and that was far from ideal.

'How can we help you, Mr Andino?'

Thank goodness she could get to the point.

'I've come to see how things are going down here. There seems to be a bigger team than yesterday. I've been dealing with a Mr Georgiou.'

'He's still around, but he called the museum in Athens and they called me.'

This wasn't news he wanted to hear, but he pressed on.

'Why? This is just a survey to get the final approvals before we build.'

She pulled a face. 'That may have been so, but we think there's a chance we'll find something.'

This was Paxos. It was hardly Olympia or Delos. 'Every archaeologist hopes to find something.'

'Well, this is more than just a hope. It's an educated guess.'

'How is that?' Really, she was meant to be the expert. But this was Paxos! He wasn't sure any ancient finds had ever been made on the small island he called home.

'Because the surveyors have found midden. And the resistivity metre shows resistance.'

'I'd be grateful if you could say that in a way that makes sense to someone who isn't an expert.' He hated the bitterness in his tone but was helpless to change it. Even his mouth tasted sour.

'Midden is traces of organic material—waste material. It shows that at some point people may have lived here.'

'Of course people have lived here. They live here now!'

She pulled a face and continued, ignoring his remark. 'And the geophysical scans show that there's something buried here.' She pointed in the direction she'd been digging. Then she repeated herself in his native Greek. Her Greek was broken, but her meaning was clear. 'Can you understand that?' she asked.

He crossed his arms. Of course he understood what she was saying, but that didn't mean he understood *why* they thought these random facts meant his hotel had to be delayed.

'I don't see how either of those things prove anything at all.'

'They don't. But they do mean we need to check further. And the Ministry of Culture isn't signing this permit until I tell them they can.'

Her. The decision for whether his hotel—or rather, his brother's hotel—went ahead or not was all down to her, the woman he'd left behind all those years ago? He couldn't decide if it was ironic or simply crazy.

Of course, he hadn't known as he'd kissed her goodbye that morning that it would be the last time he'd see her. If he had, he might not have had the courage to leave. It had been hard enough to unwrap himself from her on a normal day, but that day had turned out to be anything but normal. That day everything in his world had changed when his grandmother had called to tell him about his brother's accident. And that his two-year-old niece and nephew had been orphaned.

On the trip back to Paxos he had made an oath that he wasn't going to regret the life that he wasn't going to lead. Returning to Paxos to raise his niece and nephew was not what he would've chosen for himself, but it was a life chosen for him. He knew then that the only way to allow himself to dedicate his life to the care of his new family was to give up the dreams he'd had for himself. Some people might call it repressed, but he called it common sense and self-preservation. Paxos and the family hotel empire was going to be his life, so there was no point wishing for things that could simply never be.

Rose ignored his silent reminiscences and continued, 'If we don't find anything, it won't take long, probably just a few months.'

'A few months?' The excavators—of the large, mechanical variety—were due to start in three weeks. And after them the builders and everyone else. The new wing of the hotel was due to open nine months from now, by the following early summer.

'This isn't meant to be an excavation, just a survey. I was doing the right thing.'

'Yes, and the right thing in this instance is to let me and my team do a proper excavation. It's actually very exciting.' Her eyes widened and brightened. 'There have been some amazing Bronze Age finds in the Ionians in the past twenty years, and looking at this—'

'Bronze Age?' He wasn't the expert but the Bronze Age had ended more than half a millennium before the age of classical Greece. Finding ruins from classical Greece was unlikely. But finding something from the Bronze Age? Was she serious?

'Yes, the Bronze Age. The *Odyssey*, the *Iliad*. Homer.'

'You think you're going to find another Troy? Here?'

'Of course not, but the Ionian islands were the birthplace of Odysseus; they've found a royal palace on Ithaca and more treasure in Pylos. These islands were important in ancient times. There's every reason to believe we will find something. Odysseus' palace…a temple, for instance.'

Alessandro laughed. He hadn't meant to laugh as loudly as he had but what she was suggesting was plainly ridiculous.

'Odysseus? You want to find the three-thousand-year-old palace of a man who didn't exist?' He didn't add, 'Be my guest,' because her face had already hardened.

He looked over at Gabriel, whose eyes had grown wider during the course of their conversation. Alessandro had to make her see what she suggested was not only futile but that, if she persisted, it would throw his plans for the new hotel into doubt. Not only that, it would also jeopardise so many other businesses on the island. Paxos depended on tourists, and if there was nowhere for them to stay then the bars, restaurants and boat-tour operators would have no customers.

'Can I speak to you in private?' he said.

'Why?'

'To speak about this in a civilised manner.'

'I'm being civil now. So are you. We couldn't be more civil.'

'Let's talk in my office. We'll see if we can come to some sort of arrangement. Apart from anything else, we can get in from the sun. Have a cool drink.'

Her eyes flickered. He had her. It was mid-afternoon; the day was at its hottest and Rose, he remembered, much as she loved the Mediterranean, was still a redhead from England who had a tendency to wilt in the hot sun.

'Iced water, iced tea, *visinada*?'

She narrowed her eyes. He had her.

'All right then, lead on.'

CHAPTER TWO

NOW THEY WERE ALONE, her palms were slick with
sweat. That promised cold drink had better mate-
rialise or she'd have lost her home-ground advantage for nothing. It was difficult enough speaking
to a hotel developer who plainly didn't want her
to excavate; speaking to an old flame was another
thing entirely. It was probably best they didn't
have this conversation in front of her team.

She followed him up the hill and towards what
she knew was the Aster hotel. It was just the sort
of place she loved: a low rise, rambling affair surrounded with lush gardens. It looked more like
a small village, rather than one of those multi-
storey high-rise glass-and-concrete affairs that
had been popping up in some places. She hoped
he wasn't going to build one of those monstrosi-
ties. Paxos should retain its authentic, traditional
charm and atmosphere.

They didn't speak as they walked, but how
long could they put this conversation off? Not
the conversation about how he didn't want her

to dig up his land—the other one. The one about how he'd left her waiting, in the white dress she'd bought especially for him, and left town without telling her.

He didn't lead her to a hotel reception or foyer, but to what looked like a large house with several entrances. He took her to a blue door, unlocked it and showed her in.

Coming out of the bright sun, it took her eyes a moment to adjust, but the cold air washed over her instantly like the touch of a welcome friend. She sighed loudly, instantly regretting how pleased she sounded. The first thing she noticed when she opened her eyes was Alessandro looking down at her, grinning.

It was still difficult to reconcile the man standing before her now with the one she'd known as a student. That man had possessed a mop of curly dark hair, befitting the cash-strapped student she'd thought he was. His features had been half-hidden behind his hair and the stubble on his face. He'd dressed in worn jeans and old T-shirts.

This man was sharply groomed, his hair now short, most of the curls cut away and only the hint of a wave remaining. His face was clean shaven, which exaggerated his strong jaw and full lips. He dressed business-like—at least as business-like as anyone on the islands ever did. He wore trousers that had been recently ironed and a white shirt was tucked into them. The only nod to the location was the top button of his shirt undone and the absence of a tie.

This man was revealed to the world. The other, she now realised, had been hiding behind something.

'Can I get you a water? Or *visinada*? It's a sour cherry drink.'

'I know what it is,' she mumbled. They had drunk it together as they had walked the streets of Monastiraki. He didn't remember anything about their past connection.

Because it wasn't important to him.

'Water would be fine, please.'

She'd expected to find a house behind the pretty blue door but it was a large, modern office, far larger than any found in a university. It looked out over a garden and, in the distance, the blue waters of the sea.

Alessandro walked into an adjoining room and she manoeuvred her body to get a better look. In the next room were more desks, and she heard some voices speaking in Greek. She could tell the people were greeting Alessandro, but couldn't make out his reply. Moments later he returned, caught her looking, grinned again and handed her a cold glass.

Her hands wrapped around it gratefully and she sipped. Alessandro shut the door to the adjoining offices with an audible click.

'Have a seat.' He motioned to a sleek leather couch with a matching chair.

If she sat on the couch, would he sit next to her? Would he feel the same? Did he smell the same? She wanted to touch him. She barely trusted herself not to.

But no. He was a liar, so keeping some physical distance between Alessandro and her was a priority. She might be over him—heck, she had reason to loathe him—but what if her body hadn't got the message? Even now, something was bubbling up inside her, a need she had to suppress. She chose the chair and he raised an eyebrow.

Right.

The chair was probably where he sat. Good.

She sat, back upright, clutching the cool drink, which was now noticeably warmer in her hot hands.

'So, you want to excavate the site?' he began.

'I *am* excavating the site.'

'But this is a survey only, to finalise the approvals.'

'It may have started out like that, but the Ministry isn't going to certify it as clear to build on now.'

'Why not?'

'I told you. The surveyors have found midden. That's traces of organic material.'

'There's organic material everywhere. People live here.'

'But we can tell this is older. It suggests some

sort of waste dump. It means we need to check further. And the resistivity meter—it's a geophysical scanner the surveyor uses—has shown something under the ground that isn't soil.'

'But that could be from any time.'

'Yes, of course. It could be some bricks from a couple of hundred years ago. It could be a slab of concrete from the war. But it also could be an Iron Age dwelling. A Bronze Age temple.'

He shook his head. 'That's just so unlikely.'

'Maybe. But…' She thought of a way to explain it. 'Car accidents are not very likely, but the consequences are terrible, which is why we wear seatbelts.'

His face changed. From open and argumentative, it shut down. His entire body froze and the air in the room shifted.

Figuring he understood her analogy, she continued. 'So we're starting where the meter shows resistance.'

Alessandro stood then, turned and walked to his desk. He kept his back to her and looked at the back wall of his office for a long time.

He's thinking, that's all. He's probably been planning this new hotel for a while. Stay professional.

Finally, he turned back to her, his eyes looking slightly red. 'You cannot be serious.'

His scepticism was starting to get annoying. Or

was it simply him? Him and his strong jaw, immovable shoulders and general air of entitlement.

A developer? Alessandro Andino, a hotel developer, destroyer of ancient ruins?

She had been even more deceived by him than she'd thought.

'I am serious. You don't have a choice.'

'They said the survey would take two weeks at most.'

'Yes, two weeks to determine whether a more thorough investigation is needed. They've determined that a further investigation is needed and that's why I'm here.'

He began to pace but did not look at her. She couldn't help wondering if his indignant reaction was because of the situation in general or because it was her sitting here, telling him the bad news.

'The expansion is to support the island. Everyone here depends on tourism in some way for their livelihoods.'

'I appreciate that, I do, but—'

'It isn't just about me,' he said. 'My family's depending on this development for their futures.'

Family.

The word hit her with the force of a sledgehammer.

The kids she'd seen him with… The children who'd already been born when he'd first walked up to Rose in that bar in Athens.

How many kids did he have now? Who was

their mother? Was she still around? Had he been cheating on her when he'd been with Rose? These were the questions she'd once asked over and over until she'd realised none of it mattered. Because he'd left her.

She felt slightly faint. Hopefully that was just the heat. She downed her water and it almost came straight back up again. It was ridiculous that her body was reacting like this; her self-imposed physical-distance rule was now more important than ever.

It wasn't important that Alessandro had a wife, a family; not in the scheme of things. She was fighting for three-thousand-year-old history. She had to stay focused.

'Like I said, I do appreciate your difficulties,' she said at last. 'But we have to excavate this site.'

He sighed and scraped his dark hair off his high forehead. Were cheek bones like that even legal? He had dark hair and eyes so intense they could slice through every last ounce of common sense and self-preservation she possessed. 'How long will it take?'

'It depends. If we don't find anything, a few months. If we do, five to ten years. If we're fully funded.'

Alessandro stood. 'Five to ten years! Fully funded! I can't wait five to ten years, and I certainly can't fund a team of archaeologists.'

He'd deceived her and now he was going to get

in the way of what could be the greatest achieve-
ment of her career. She loathed him—she shouldn't
be wondering how he smelt or thinking about running a fingertip along his now bare jawline.

'No one's asking you to fund it. Try and see it
from a broader perspective—we might find something that's been hidden for thousands of years.'

He placed his face in his palms, and for a brief
moment she felt some sympathy for someone who
had made such an investment and was having his
plans thrown into chaos.

'We might not find anything.'

'But if you do I can pretty much kiss goodbye
to my plans. The children's futures, the island's
future.'

Children. The family he'd left Rose for. Just as
her father had.

She pushed the feelings of rejection deeper
down, to where even she couldn't see them. She
had a job to do here and it couldn't matter that the
man now standing before her was the one who
had once broken her heart.

'It's important,' she said. 'It's very important
to preserve the past and learn from it.'

'The future's important too, you know. The
people living now. Tourism's the biggest indus-
try on Paxos. The hotel wouldn't only support
my family, it would support the entire island.
You live in the past but I'm concerned about the
present—the people who need to feed and clothe

their children, the people who need to buy medicine for their parents.'

'I understand that.'

'But do you? History is important. I know we need to preserve our culture. But we also need to eat.'

'When we find the ruins, it will bring tourists.'

'This isn't Troy. You can't honestly think you'll find something with a connection to Homer.'

Most people accepted that Homer's hero, Odysseus, had never existed, and the hope of finding something definitively related to him was next to impossible. But finding traces of Bronze Age civilisation in this area from the time of the Trojan war was a real possibility. It would change conventional thinking about Greek history and would be a career-defining discovery for Rose. Alessandro's patronising doubt was more than irritating. It was hurtful.

'One more month—four weeks. That's all I can offer. And then the builders will have to start.'

'That's silly.'

'Why is it silly?'

'Because when we find some ruins you'll just have to knock it all down again.'

'You won't find any ruins.'

She laughed. 'You know, I remember your tenacity, but I don't remember your condescension.'

He stopped pacing mid-stride.

This was the first time either had acknowledged their past. Until now it had simply rippled, unseen, beneath the surface.

'I'm not being condescending; I've lived here most of my life, and I promise you will not find anything. And certainly not anything from the Bronze Age.'

She scoffed, shook her head and paused, doubtful. 'What makes you so sure?'

'Because my family has lived in this village for over a hundred years, our ancestors for a millennium. If anything to do with Homer or Odysseus was on this island, we'd know about it. My family would know, the locals would know. There would be rumours, stories about it. And there are none!'

Oh, this man was the limit. Abandoning her in Athens, lying about having children and now being the one person trying to get in the way of her and a career-critical discovery.

Even if they didn't find something as old as the Bronze Age, the experts who had surveyed this site believed there was something here. Something worthy of further investigation. And how long would it take? If they found something, then it could take years to properly search the whole site. But she knew, as much as Alessandro did, that the museum was not going to lend her this team for ever. That eventually they would certify the site as free to build on if they didn't find anything. She didn't have years, she had a couple of months at most. Probably less.

'Three months. If we don't find anything in three months, then we'll leave.' That would give her plenty of time to investigate the area of interest.

'Three months! Impossible. You have six weeks.'

In all likelihood the museum would recall the team before then anyway. But she wasn't about to tell Alessandro that. Six weeks would probably be sufficient to check what the survey team had identified but, no matter what, she could control whether the permit was signed.

'Six weeks—fine. From today.' She thought she saw him wince. 'And if, when, we find something, then as long as it takes.'

'Fine,' he said through gritted teeth.

She put down her glass and stood. He held out a broad hand to seal their deal. Again, she hesitated. Even the thought of skin-to-skin contact made her body tingle. What would happen if they did actually touch?

He was taken, a family man. Probably a married man. So what if a handshake stirred something inside her? There was no possibility of anything more than a handshake happening between them. So she held out her hand and he wrapped his around hers.

Oh, no. It was a mistake. When his large hand enveloped hers she felt it in her belly. After the obligatory second, she pulled her hand out of his and stepped back.

While she didn't feel as though she'd won, this

was the best deal she was going to get. And, more importantly, she could get out of this blasted office.

It was so unlike the life she'd imagined for him. There were bookcases full of books about management. Several large, shiny computer screens. And yet there were still traces of the man she had known just the same—a beautiful globe of the earth, modern painting, an African sculpture.

She should turn and leave, but she hesitated. She'd moved on with her life and, until an hour ago, she would have told anyone who asked that her life was just fine, thank you very much. She knew she should have let this lie; it would only aggravate Alessandro's and her already tense professional relationship.

Was there any point asking? His answer wouldn't change anything. Bringing it up would only inflame an old wound. She'd already wasted too many hours trying to use logic to come up with a reason that could possibly excuse Alessandro's behaviour. There were plenty of explanations—but none that would ever be enough. If he'd really loved her as he'd claimed, he would've told her that he had children. He wouldn't have lied.

What if it's your only chance?

The question came out in a rush, not dignified, not even calm. 'Why didn't you tell me about your children?'

He rubbed his face with his palm. 'I couldn't.'

'Why not? It's easy—"I have kids". People say that all the time.'

He looked down at nothing in particular on his black boot. 'I thought it was best.'

'Best for you, you mean.' Her tone was bitter, but she didn't care. All the hurt, the pain and the confusion of that time was resurfacing and she was powerless to stop it. It was mortifying. She should have been over him years ago.

'No. I didn't tell you because I thought it was best you didn't know.'

She scoffed. 'Yes, it's much easier to seduce someone if you lie about having a family.'

'No, Rose, it wasn't like that. I didn't want to ruin your life too.'

'What are you even talking about? You did hurt me.' Her heart was racing in her throat and her hands were shaking. This wasn't how this had been meant to go. She hadn't meant to let him know how much he had hurt her. She should leave before she said anything else.

'I didn't mean to, honestly. If there had been any other way... Please believe me.'

'If you weren't free to have a relationship, you should have told me from the beginning.'

'I was free. When we met.'

'You expect me to believe you didn't know about your children?'

'Yes, I knew about them. But, Rose, they aren't mine.'

CHAPTER THREE

ROSE LAUGHED, a sad, cynical laugh. 'You just called them your children; I saw pictures... I can't believe a single thing you say, can I?'

'They are my children, for all intents and purposes. But by blood they are my niece and nephew.'

His answer knocked the breath out of her. He'd had an older brother... Alessandro hadn't told her much about him, nor about the rest of his family.

'Your brother's children?'

Alessandro nodded.

'What happened to your brother?'

'He was killed with his wife in a car crash.'

The pieces clicked into place.

'The day you left Athens.' It was a statement not a question. She was as sure of that as she was sure she would find ancient ruins beneath this island.

He stared at her for an age, jaw set, eyes hard, before he finally, slowly, lowered his dark head in a quiet nod.

She exhaled several breaths loudly.

'That's why you came back here? That's why you really left Athens so suddenly?'

He nodded again.

'Oh, Alessandro, why didn't you just tell me?'

'I had to leave quickly.'

That was plausible and yet…

'The twins. They were two years old,' he continued.

'When their parents were killed?'

He nodded as though he didn't trust himself to speak. She didn't blame him. She was finding it hard to speak herself.

'Oh, Alessandro, I don't know what to say.'

He waved her attempt at sympathy away and her heart broke a little more. She felt helpless. She wanted to reach out and touch him, hug him, but no—touch was impossible.

In all the scenarios she'd imagined, all the reasons she'd dreamt up for him leaving, none of them had involved a family tragedy that necessitated him rushing back home.

In almost every scenario he had simply chosen to leave her. Had rejected her.

She'd assumed the worst of him.

Did that say as much about her insecurities as it did about him? She knew that her father's abandonment had scarred her, but had it affected her to the point that she couldn't believe someone might have a different, even innocent, explanation for leaving?

No. Alessandro had told her, point blank, their lives were on different paths. He hadn't told her about his brother. And she'd seen the photos of him and the kids.

It wasn't her fault she hadn't known the truth.

'You still could have told me.'

He was still studying his shoe, looking out of the window, looking at anything but her.

'There was no need to tell you.'

'Yeah, I get it. I was just a fling. There was no need to tell me anything about you.'

'No, Rose, no.' He went to her now, his eyes urgent. He wrapped his hand around her elbow and the world shrank to just the two of them. Warmth spread up her arm, to her shoulder and her chest.

'No. I didn't tell you because I knew you, I knew your dreams for the future. I knew you didn't want to be stuck on a tiny island with me raising two kids who weren't your own. I didn't *want* to lie to you.'

'Where are the twins now? They must be...' She did a quick calculation. 'Fourteen or fifteen years old.'

'They turn sixteen next week. They live here, with me and my grandmother.'

'You raised them?'

'With my *yiayia*, yes.'

It was a lot to take in.

It sounded noble, but he still could have told her. 'All these years I believed you'd just rejected me, walked out on me. I assumed there was another woman. I assumed...' She couldn't even say it aloud.

I assumed that everything you'd told me was a lie. I assumed I wasn't good enough.

'I would have understood; it would have...'

It would have eased the pain.

She shook her head; she wasn't ready to admit the pain he'd caused her.

'I did what I thought was best. For you.'

'It's pretty presumptuous for you to decide what's best for me.'

'We were so close, it was so hard for me to leave you. It would've been harder if you'd had to leave me too.'

'I don't understand what you mean.'

He ran his hands through his dark hair, the gesture making it stick up and look slightly wild.

'Because you didn't want the life that I was destined for. You wanted to travel, be a free spirt, explore the world. You didn't want to be the wife of a businessman, stuck in the one place.'

He was right. They'd spoken about this in Athens when they'd discussed their dreams and wishes for the future. Her dream had never included comfortable domesticity.

'I couldn't bear to hear you tell me that you didn't want to spend your life with me.'

'You still could have asked.' Her voice was quiet.

He placed his hands on his hips. 'And what would you have said?'

'I would have…' *I would have wanted to be with you.* One question they had never asked one another—indeed, one question she had never asked herself—was, what would she have given up to be with him?

And she didn't know the answer.

'I would have had a difficult decision to make. But we could have made it together. Unless…' The chill slipped down her spine despite the summer heat. 'Unless you simply didn't want to be with me.'

Alessandro looked down.

Right. She had been right all along. He might have had a better excuse for not contacting her than she had ever believed, but the reason he'd left was still the same.

He didn't want a future with her.

Not then.

Not now.

CHAPTER FOUR

ROSE KICKED THE ground as she made her way back to the dig. The dig that would, hopefully, jeopardise his new plans. And put the livelihoods of half the island at risk. Ruin his niece's and nephew's future.

Gah! He was trying to guilt her into abandoning the search and that was not going to work. She would not feel guilty about it; there was a possibility of a world-changing historical find.

Admittedly, the chance wasn't great, but the rewards if she did find something would be remarkable. Not material wealth—she didn't care much for that—but the thrill of discovering something, figuring out what it was and learning from it. The chance to shape what everyone knew about the history of ancient Greece? That was priceless.

Gabriel looked up when she arrived back. 'Is everything okay?'

'I sorted it,' Rose replied. 'He's not happy we're here, but he doesn't have much of a choice. He's given us six weeks.'

'Six weeks? And what if we're not finished?' Gabriel gave her a doubting look.

'Look, let's cross that bridge when we come to it.'

She didn't tell him about her suspicion that the museum might cut off their funding well before that if they hadn't made any progress. But if they found something, even something small, then the museum might have more influence with Alessandro. She wouldn't get too far ahead of herself and concentrate on the present.

They had divided the area into portions and were concentrating on one section at a time, removing each layer of sediment carefully. So far, she estimated they had removed about nearly a quarter of a ton of dirt and this might just be the beginning. But with every trowel-full, every scrape, every bucket load, there was a little hope.

Rose worked until the light faded and she could work no more, as she tended to do when she was in the middle of a project. She found it hard to stop when she was in the flow. She'd have to look into getting some lights rigged up to extend her working hours. Particularly as she was running against the clock.

When the light and her team had gone, she walked back to the room where she was staying. She was sharing it with two younger women, students who were part of the team. They were lying on their bunks chatting about some men they'd met the night before.

Good luck to them. She wanted to stop them and warn them against a summer romance, lest the subject of that romance turn up in their lives over a decade later and throw them into a spin.

But she didn't.

She took a quick shower to wash the dust of the day away. Clean but hungry, she took her laptop down to the taverna her landlady, Myra, had recommended. She ordered a glass of white wine and a plate of stuffed grape leaves, fried aubergine and tzatziki and looked up Alessandro Andino online.

And this time she didn't close her laptop lid at the first photo of Alessandro with the two children but read everything carefully.

It was all true.

Alessandro Andino was the Managing Director of Aster Hotels, a hotel chain stretching over the Ionian Islands and down the west coast of Greece. The brand was famous for its luxury eco-friendly hotels and boutique resorts that gave the guests the full Greek island experience without the partying and the crowds. It was a family business, established by Alessandro's grandfather and run in turn by his father and then his brother.

She'd heard of Aster Hotels—she'd even stayed in one in Santorini once—but she'd never realised they were owned by Alessandro's family.

Why would she know? He hadn't mentioned it. All he'd told her was that his parents were dead.

There seemed to be a lot of things Alessandro hadn't mentioned about his family.

She found a recent feature on him in a glossy magazine. It related the story of the tragic death of his brother and sister-in-law. A semi-trailer had crossed to the wrong side of the road, killing them both instantly and leaving their two-year-old twins orphaned in an instant. Alessandro had dedicated himself to raising the twins and running the hotel empire. The article spoke about his game-changing ideas and how his practices were influencing other operators to rethink the hospitality business in a sustainable way, not just in Greece but all over the world.

He had been successful and influential.

But it was not the life she had imagined for him.

It was not the life he'd imagined for himself.

He hadn't lied to her about his passions. The relief she felt at that was still marred by the fact that he hadn't been completely open with her either. He still could have told her about his brother. She didn't know what she would have done, but he shouldn't have left her without an explanation.

The customers in the taverna came and went around her. The wooden table was covered in a checked blue-and-white cloth. She sat inside, but next to a window that opened out onto the small square and other tables. The place was lit up with lanterns and smelt of candles and seafood. She bit into her fried aubergine with a satisfying crunch and her mouth filled with soft goodness.

Would it have made any difference, knowing what had happened to him? It would've saved her all the speculation, all the hurt. Yes, the pain would have been less acute if he'd told her he was leaving her to raise his niece and nephew, and not two children of his own he hadn't told her about.

You might have followed him.

Maybe. She was so in love with him, consumed by him. In the crazy storm of new love, who knew what she might have given up to be with him?

Maybe *he* was right. That by leaving without a word he'd been doing her a favour and saving her from having to make the decision. He knew she wasn't looking to settle down, help him raise twins on a small Greek island and run a hotel chain. But, with him knowing what he knew about her, she might have felt obliged to. And then there was that comment he'd made that even now she couldn't quite understand.

It was so hard for me to leave you. It would've been harder if you'd had to leave me too.

What on earth had he meant by that? Had he meant that by sparing her the decision, he had spared her having to break up with him? He'd also spared himself having to be dumped by her. That wasn't a real excuse; he must have known he was hurting her. No matter how noble he thought he was being, he should have discussed the matter with her. He could dress it up however he wanted, but he'd still been untruthful.

She groaned quietly to herself.

Thinking about him, her limbs tingled even now. The sensation of his voice was like the best chocolate melting on her tongue, sliding through her body. The last vestiges of his youthful roundness had slipped away over the years, leaving his jaw lean, his cheekbones defined and his eyes steely. Responsibility had made his back straighter, his shoulders squared and his demeanour determined. And yet…for a few brief moments, when he'd laughed or when he'd grinned and shrugged, she'd caught a glimpse of the Alessandro she had known. And loved.

No matter his reason, he'd still made the decision without her and that was not what couples did, was it? If he had truly and properly loved her he would have told her he was leaving and why.

He'd left her, abandoned her for another family. Just as her father had.

Knowing that he had a good reason for leaving didn't change anything; they still didn't have a future. Alessandro's life was here, raising his niece and nephew and running a string of hotels. Further, he had plans to extend one of those hotels.

On the same ground where her ruins might lie.

Their lives were still heading in opposite directions. He was determined to build this hotel, no matter what she might find. And he was determined she would not get in his way.

'What's the matter, Ali?' Alessandro's grandmother asked him that evening at dinner.

He made a point of joining his grandmother, Lucas and Ana every evening when he was at home. Business often took him elsewhere but he looked forward to these evenings with just the four of them. Yiayia didn't cook a lot any more, and he'd hired a housekeeper, Angelina, to help them all out during the day, but in the evenings it was just family.

'Nothing's the matter,' he replied.

'You're quiet this evening. And Ana said you looked furious this afternoon when you brought a pretty redhead into your office. The one who is staying in the village at Myra's.'

Alessandro looked at his niece. She was smirking.

'The redhead…' He didn't repeat 'pretty'. Apart from anything, 'pretty' didn't accurately describe her. Rose was more than pretty—she was beautiful. Heart-in-the-throat, jaw-to-the-ground beautiful. 'Is an archaeologist who wants to fully excavate the site we're building on.'

'But she is pretty?' his grandmother said.

'Yiayia, it doesn't matter what she looks like, she's trying to stop the new build.'

'Ah, so she is, then. But they have to do a survey. It's the law.'

'Yes, but it was just meant to be a survey. A formality.' Theo wouldn't have waited until the last minute to get the survey. Theo would have been onto it earlier. Theo, the brilliant business-man. Theo, the favourite son. Theo had never been the disappointment Alessandro always was. 'And now she wants to dig deeper. She wants to hold up the build with a full excavation. She thinks she's going to find ruins from the Bronze Age. She thinks she's going to find something from Homer.'

'Wow! That would be amazing,' Ana said, and he shot her a glare.

'First, she's not going to find anything. That's patently absurd, for so many reasons. The main one being that Homer's stories are fictional. Odysseus, Helen of Troy…none of them existed.'

'You're a bit worked up,' Lucas added.

His pulse had been unpredictable since he'd seen Rose that afternoon. It was now punching out a loud nightclub beat in his temples. It didn't help that his family, the very people he was doing all this for, were not on his side. He rubbed his forehead but found no relief.

'Of course I'm worked up. The whole project is being delayed by this nonsense.'

His family looked at him silently. His heart sometimes caught in his throat when he looked at the children. He didn't know how a real parent could have loved two kids more. The two toddlers he'd found on his return to Paxos were now young adults, tall, long-limbed and unaware of how beautiful youth looked on them. He was doing this for them to protect their inheritance, to give them everything their parents should have given them. To prove that, even though he'd made mistakes, he wasn't a complete disappointment to the family.

'Don't you all care? I'm doing this all for you. For the island. So you children have a future here.'

He didn't add, *It was your father's dream to extend this hotel, the first Aster Hotel.*

Alessandro had waited years for a chance to buy the land that bordered the existing hotel. Theo had always dreamed of extending the Andino offering on Paxos. Alessandro owed this to the village, to the people who had supported his family and him when tragedy had struck them. The people of Ninos had rallied round and helped Yiayia and him raise the twins.

'We care, we care,' they mumbled and looked at their plates.

'We know what you do for us.' Yiayia rubbed his arm. 'You just seem… I don't know. You've handled stress before, but you don't usually look like this.'

'Like what?' he snapped.

'Like you might bite our heads off.'

He looked at his niece and nephew properly. Ana was watching him, questions filling her beautiful dark eyes. Lucas's focus was firmly on his plate and his food.

He loved these children with all his heart. While taking on his brother's kids had certainly not been part of his grand plan, it had been the greatest privilege and pleasure of his life to get to raise them and love them.

They were bright, dynamic and funny, even when they were challenging; he loved them with all his heart. These children had soothed his heart and reminded him why he had made the right decision all those years ago in not telling Rose that he was leaving.

Despite what she thought, he *had* wanted a future with her. For several glorious weeks in a balmy Athens summer he had thought of nothing but being with Rose, loving Rose, spending his life with her.

But it wasn't to be. And he had saved her from a choice that would have ended up hurting one of them, one way or another. She might not have known it then, and she might not realise it now, but by leaving her he'd ensured she had the life she wanted, the career she loved. He wasn't responsible for ruining her dreams or her life. She hadn't had to give up the career she wanted to fulfil a duty. They way he had.

'There is nothing more important than your family.' His father's last words to him still echoed in Alessandro's ears, even after all this time.

He pushed back his chair and picked up his plate.

'I just need some air. I'm going for a walk.'

While he would never admit that Rose was his destination, he wasn't surprised when his feet led him to Myra's B&B. Myra smiled and said, 'Oh yes, she's very pretty. She's gone to Joe's. You can probably find her there most evenings.'

Alessandro thanked her and she waved after him, yelling at him to, 'Have a good evening. Don't do anything I wouldn't do!' before dissolving into laughter.

These people… It was not just his own family but the others in the village who were fixated on the fact that Rose was pretty. Very pretty. Couldn't they see she was out to destroy the plans for the island? If Rose got her way, the site for his new hotel would be a muddy dirt pit for the next decade. Myra's B&B might do a fine trade, but his hotel would bring even more opportunities for everyone. More tourists would mean more restaurants, cafés and tavernas; more boat operators, more shops.

And more shops, restaurants and boat operators would mean more customers for Myra too.

Ana's words had shaken him the most. She was

excited about the prospect of Rose finding some ruins on their land, even knowing it would halt the plans to build the hotel. And, if his own family were seduced by the idea, others would be too.

He had to do more than just sit on his hands and wait out the next six weeks. Even if finding anything remotely connected to Homer was impossible, she might find something else. Greece was littered with ancient ruins, and someone doing the survey had clearly thought there was something interesting lurking down there. Discovery of anything more than a couple of hundred years' old could put an end to the whole project.

The land had not been cheap. The build itself was going to be expensive as well; architecturally designed for energy efficiency, using recycled, repurposed material. The money wasn't the only thing: he would lose a significant portion of the children's inheritance, but he might be able to use some of his money to make it up. But expanding the hotel had been his father's plan and Theo's dream. The plan he'd talked about since Arianna had first become pregnant with the twins.

We must leave them a legacy on Paxos. They must have a home here always.

He had a family legacy to protect and he needed a plan.

The plan hadn't come to him by the time he entered Joe's, but no doubt it would when he saw her.

No such luck.

Rose was sitting in a booth near a window, laptop in front of her. Unlike this afternoon, when her hair had been tied back in a loose bun, it was now loose and flowed around her shoulders in thick, amber waves that caught the candlelight.

Beautiful.

Even that word didn't do her justice.

He remembered the first time he'd seen her. He'd literally frozen on the spot mid-turn on his way out of a lecture theatre.

'Alessandro!' Joe called, regrettably alerting Rose to his presence. She shut her laptop lid as soon as she saw him.

Interesting.

There was something on her screen she didn't want him to see. No doubt she had been checking out his story about his dead brother, his orphaned family.

She hadn't known before today, he realised with a pang that felt a bit like guilt. No, he had nothing to feel guilty about! He had raised his brother's orphaned twins. He had run the hotel chain to hand over to them one day.

The Andino family, while successful, liked to keep a reasonably low profile and he was particularly careful about keeping the children out of the press as much as he could. A recent interview he'd given to a magazine was the first time he'd openly discussed his brother's death. But maybe, he allowed, he had assumed that at some point

Rose would have figured out the truth, almost as though he'd been expecting her to turn up one day.

You've been waiting for her.

Yes, maybe at the beginning he had wondered if she would turn up on his doorstep, angry at him for not telling her why he had left, having figured it out.

But no. The plan had been for her not to figure it out. The plan had been for her to be able to get on with her life. Not have it interrupted, like his had been.

You were not honest with her. You can hardly blame her. Maybe you just aren't as famous as you think you are.

He had looked her up, many times, on those days he was feeling particularly low. On the anniversary. When an important deal fell through. When Yiayia was unwell. He knew that she'd earned her doctorate, been involved in several significant discoveries and published well-received papers. She was living the life she had always planned.

He hadn't been able to learn much about her personal life; she'd kept that very private. But photos he had seen of her with other men—maybe colleagues, maybe lovers—had made his stomach churn.

Alessandro asked Joe for a drink for himself and another for Rose. He walked to her table. 'May I join you?'

She slipped her laptop into her bag and motioned to the spare chair.

'You were working late,' he said.

'I've got a lot to do. I've only got six weeks.' She smiled at him and he felt it warm his bones. 'I'm going to order some lights in, which will give us more time. We're lucky it's summer, so we have more daylight, but it would be good to get in a few extra hours at each end of the day.'

She was seriously determined. For a moment he wondered if her ambition would be too much for him.

Joe brought over the drinks. Rose picked up her glass and touched it gently to his.

'To old times.'

'Old times,' he repeated, and the memory of those times flooded back: hot nights, sweaty sheets, entangled fingers; promises.

'Your niece and nephew, what are their names?'

Her question shook him back to the present. 'Lucas and Ana.'

'Lovely. Tell me about them.'

The muscles in his shoulders unclenched a little. They weren't going argue, they were just going to talk, like old friends catching up.

'Well, they're teenagers. Full of hormones and angst and belief they're ready to run the world.'

She smiled. 'That sounds about right. Has it been terribly hard, raising them on your own?'

'I haven't been on my own completely. My

grandmother's always been there. And everyone
in the village—everyone on the island, really.
My family's lived here for generations; everyone
knew my brother and his wife. Everyone wanted
to help me.'

This was true, and yet the financial and emo-
tional burden had fallen primarily to him. He'd always known his grandmother wouldn't be around
for ever and then Lucas and Ana would only have
him. Another reason why it was so important that
he left them comfortably set up for the future.

Not that he had any intention of leaving them,
but he did have other family businesses, other
hotels, to manage.

'And you? Tell me about you. I thought you
wanted to travel. Write.'

He shrugged. He'd almost forgotten those am-
bitions. He'd buried them deep when his life had
abruptly changed direction.

It wasn't all bad; he was healthy and raising
two delightful children with his grandmother. As
far as life sentences went, he could have done a
lot worse. And it turned out he was good at running a business. He might not have been as good
as his brother, but he'd done all right. He even, as
it turned out, enjoyed it. Who would have known?
Not his father, that was for sure.

*You're a disappointment, why can't you be as
responsible as your brother?*

Instead of fading with the years, his father's

criticisms were as loud in Alessandro's head as ever. Probably because the hotel extension was at risk. The family's legacy on Paxos was at risk.

'I'm boring,' he said. 'I've been living here raising two kids, keeping a hotel business running. I'm sure you've been doing much more interesting things. Tell me what you've been up to.'

Tell me if you have a boyfriend. Tell me if you're married. Tell me if you have children. He wasn't going ask those questions outright. He wasn't sure he wanted to know the answer.

'Are you still based in Birmingham?'

'I'm in London, actually, but I don't spend a lot of time there.'

That sounded about right. Rose never wanted to be tied down; she always wanted to be ready to find the next discovery.

'After I finished my PhD, I spent some time in Istanbul. Since then I've been travelling wherever opportunities arise—Sicily and then southern Spain.'

'It sounds amazing,' he said, regretting the wistfulness in his voice.

The day he'd received the phone call from his grandmother to tell him about the accident, he'd made the decision not to dwell on a life he wouldn't lead. He hadn't contacted Rose because he hadn't wanted her to feel as though she had to join him. He hadn't wanted two careers to be destroyed that day. Two sets of dreams.

But also because talking to her might just have caused him to break the oath he'd made to dedicate himself to his family. To look after his niece and nephew and to prove to his father that he wasn't selfish. Or disloyal. That he loved his family as much as anyone.

He could feel the memory reaching back into his thoughts again. But now was not the time. He took a deep breath, but it wouldn't leave. He'd been ten, foolish, and had wanted to see how far into the ocean he could swim. Only, he hadn't figured that he'd have to swim back. It was Theo who had come to his rescue, dragging him back to the beach. He'd been freezing, close to unconsciousness, but still alert enough to feel his father shaking him and to hear his words: 'You fool, you nearly got your brother killed.'

Which was why now, after keeping that promise for all these years, he had to be strong. The reasons that kept him from Rose fifteen ago were just as strong now. He had his duty to his family, she had her career. So, even though the need to pick up her hand and press it to his lips might be so overwhelming it was causing his vision to blur, he clenched his hands under the table and simply smiled.

They finished their drink and he followed her out of the warm taverna into the night air, cooled by a fresh breeze off the sea. They stood facing one another, waiting to leave in their opposite directions. A string of coloured lights lit the square and danced across their faces.

He stood only a foot away from her and she felt her body sway towards him. His eyes were so serious and dark, but now she fancied he was smiling. Which didn't make sense.

'Goodnight,' she said, stepping back and needing to put back the distance between them. She needed to get to her room to process the events of the day.

'You should come and stay at the hotel,' he said.

She scoffed. 'I can't afford the hotel.' The Aster might appear low-key but she bet that inside was boutique luxury that earned every one of its five stars.

'I meant, stay as my guest.'

She shook her head. 'I can't do that.'

'You can and you should. For starters, you'd have your own room.'

How did he know she was bunking with the others? While she was used to sharing rooms when she travelled to places to excavate, the other two women were students and good friends. Rose felt like their sensible older sister. Or, worse, their mother.

'And you'll be closer to the site.'

'I can't impose like that. And I really can't afford to pay you for a room.' Her salary from the university was not great but sufficient for her needs. The room she had rented was basic but adequate.

'I'm inviting you as my guest. I don't expect you to pay.'

'Why?' She crossed her arms. The kids might be his niece and nephew, but she still didn't know if there was a Mrs Andino in the picture. Not that it mattered.

'All right, I do have an ulterior motive.'

Her stomach leapt and her body flushed.

'You'll be closer to the site and, with less of a commute, you'll be able to work more. Faster work means you'll be finished quicker.'

A strangely disappointing answer.

'And if you are eating all your meals at the hotel…'

'You're offering to pay for my meals too? No, Alessandro, I couldn't.'

'You keep saying "can't". But you really mean you *won't*.'

'That's true.'

She wanted to dig deeper, probe his true motivation for the invitation. Did he want to be closer to her? How much would she see of him? How far apart would their rooms be? She searched his face for answers and his dark gaze met hers.

Her stomach flipped. Could she stand to sleep so close to him every night or would it drive her to distraction?

'It's less than a five-minute walk from the hotel down to the site. It's nearly twenty minutes to up here. You'd have an extra half-hour a day at least.' His eyes didn't leave hers.

'What do you get out of it?'

'The pleasure of seeing more of you, of course.' His tone was flirtatious, but not serious.

She tore her gaze from his and pretended to laugh. 'Let's not go there.' She was serious. Alessandro was a man you only wanted to get over once and she had used up her turn.

He held up his hands. 'I don't know what you mean.'

'It'll be best for both of us, and our work, if we lay off the flirting, don't you think?'

'If that will make you more comfortable.'

She nodded.

'So is that a yes to the hotel?'

'I still don't understand why you want to help me.'

'Oh, I don't. You've misunderstood—I want you to clear that site and get out of here as soon as possible.' Despite his earlier promise, his flirtatious grin was back. 'Seriously, Rose, I'm trying to make amends for everything. I honestly didn't mean to hurt you and I honestly thought I was doing the right thing by you when I left.'

That was a good reason, she supposed. And she'd save some time each day. And have her own space. But she'd also be closer to Alessandro and she was still undecided about whether that was a good thing or not.

She nodded.

'Great. Pack up your bags and I'll have someone pick them up and bring them to the hotel tomorrow while you're working. And tomorrow evening I'd like to show you around Paxos.'

Doubt stirred in her belly along with something else—danger.

'But why?'

He looked down at her and this time his eyes were serious. 'I am truly, truly sorry for leaving without a word. And despite everything we are old friends. And hospitality is my business. I would like to extend the hospitality to you. You can't work twenty-four hours a day.'

'Maybe I can,' she said, still unsure about whether seeing Alessandro was the best way to spend her spare time.

'You love to eat. You can't have changed that much.'

His reference to his knowledge of her from the past threw her off-guard. She did love food. And she loved Greek food. She salivated, despite having only eaten an hour earlier.

'I do have to eat,' she admitted.

'Tomorrow night, then. Seven.'

'It's still light at seven.'

'Exactly. How can I show you around in the

dark? I'll see you tomorrow evening.' He nodded and turned before she could say anything else.

Had she just agreed to move into his hotel? And go on a date?

Her heart was beating in her throat and her body felt strange, full of nervous energy. Or something else. He'd invited her to stay at his hotel. *That's because you're working on his land and he's extending his hospitality.* His motive was probably what he said it was: to save her time and let her leave the island as soon as possible.

But what if he was motivated by something else? By the very thing that had brought them together in the first place—a deep, irresistible connection? An overwhelming attraction. No, that could never be. He'd lied to her. Maybe not in the way she'd originally thought, but she certainly couldn't trust him with her body again. Let alone her heart.

A hotel room of her own would be more comfortable than the bottom bunk she was currently sleeping on. It would also give her some space from the others working on the site.

But you'll be closer to him. You might meet his family.

And his wanting to take her to dinner and show her around the island—what could possibly be his motivation for that?

CHAPTER FIVE

ALESSANDRO SLEPT BADLY, waking every hour with some other snippet of the previous night's conversation replaying in his head. Images of Rose flashed across his mind, making his heart race and his body sweat. Her light-brown eyes were penetrating, challenging, furious.

He'd fallen asleep again and this time had seen her laughing, her mouth full and wide, her golden eyes bright. But that memory wasn't from yesterday, it was from fourteen years ago in Athens. Before he'd broken her heart.

He'd told himself she would have got over him pretty quickly. It was difficult to imagine that many good men would not have crossed her path, desperate to spend their lives with her. And he, himself, was far from perfect.

But yesterday he'd begun to doubt. Despite her best efforts, the hurt and confusion had been apparent on her face. She'd really never known why he'd left, and for the first time he'd questioned his decision to break up with her without giving her the full story.

It had been the hardest conversation of his life. It had taken him days to work up the courage to call her and say what had needed to be said. *We're on different paths, we need to go in our own directions*... His chest still ached remembering that day.

Her words from the day before gnawed at him. He hated to admit it, but she had a point: it had been easier to hide behind the excuse that he'd made a noble choice by leaving without a word. But, really, he hadn't wanted to hear her say, 'No, I won't come to you.'

Or, worse, he hadn't wanted her to come to live with them, regret it and change her mind, not only leaving him but the twins as well.

He'd never had a serious girlfriend for that very reason: the risk that the twins would become attached to her and then break their hearts if she left. The children's cries for their parents who would never return still rang in his ears. They'd been old enough to know their parents were gone, too young to understand why. He wasn't going to do that to them again. So his relationships had remained light, casual and commitment-free.

Maybe he was mad to have invited Rose to stay at the hotel. Maybe she was right to be suspicious. He did have an ulterior motive for wanting her close. But it wasn't what she thought. It wasn't to ingratiate his way back into her bed.

He would show her how important his business was. He would show her how important his family was and why he'd had to break up with her. It wasn't because he was disloyal, but just the opposite. He'd left her because he'd had to protect his family.

Two sets of eyes looked up at him when he walked into the kitchen, Yiayia's and Ana's. It was as though they knew he had something to tell them.

'I'll let Angelina know, but I've asked Rose to come and stay while she's here.'

'Here?' Yiayia asked.

'Yes, in the flat.'

'Not the hotel?'

'She's an old friend.'

His grandmother and niece exchanged looks. Their silent conversation, communicated with eyebrows and head tilts, went something like, *See, I told you he knew her.*

No, you told me he liked her.

Same difference.

Not at all!

'We will make her very comfortable,' Yiayia said aloud.

'Thank you.' Then, as an afterthought he wasn't sure how to explain, 'And you will…?'

'We'll behave,' Ana said and they both laughed.

* * *

After breakfast, he went to his office for a few teleconferences. Mid-morning his phone rang and, noticing the number was from, Demetri, his builder, his heart rate accelerated.

'So I hear you're having some difficulty getting the final approvals.'

Good news travelled fast. 'Not difficulty. There's simply been a slight delay, that's all.'

'How slight?'

'A couple of weeks. At most.' Demetri didn't need to know about the deal he'd made with Rose. He'd convince her to take her pointless search for Odysseus elsewhere in the Ionian Sea.

'You know it will throw all the suppliers out. We've got deliveries starting in two weeks. We're due to break ground in a month.'

The man's impertinence annoyed him. Who did he think he was? Alessandro was the one whose project was on the line.

'I know that,' he said through a jaw clenched as tightly as the deadline he was facing.

'So what do I tell them?'

'Who?'

'The suppliers. Should they still deliver in two weeks?'

Alessandro let out a long sigh. The steel beams might sit on the site longer than planned. Payment would be due on them. The astronomical mortgage he'd taken over the land would increase, as would the repayments. But if he didn't give the go-ahead he'd loose his window with the suppliers. Getting building material shipped from the mainland was already a nightmare. And if the build was delayed? He'd be stuck with a pile of steel frames for a few extra weeks.

'Yes, they should still deliver.'

'Can I get that in writing?'

'What? No, you cannot. My word will suffice.'

Alessandro hit 'end call' with a satisfying jab and threw the phone on his desk.

In writing? *In writing?* His word as a businessman had never been questioned. Nor had his brother's, his father's or his father's father's.

Why would this man question his?

Because you're not your father. And you're not Theo. You're the replacement. Second best. You're just the back-up, the great disappointment. The irresponsible one.

He just had to hope that Rose would finish her search sooner rather than later.

A knock at the door nudged him out of his reverie. His grandmother entered his office bearing a cup of steaming black coffee. His heart rate hadn't returned to healthy levels since his conversation with Demetri, but it was good to see her.

'Thank you, Yiayia, are you having one?'

She waved her hand dismissively. 'I've had three already. That's probably enough.'

He laughed. Three cups of her strong black coffee probably was enough for anyone, but particularly an eighty-four-year-old. As a rule, he tried not to notice that she was getting older, frailer. In the usual course of events it was easy; he stuck his head in the proverbial sand. But some days, such as if he'd just returned from a trip away, her frailty hit him like a gut punch.

She still has years to go.

Yet the rest of his family had all died young. His own mother had passed way after a short fight with cancer when he'd only been four—barely older than Ana and Lucas had been when their mother had died. And his father had suffered a stroke when Alessandro had been fifteen. Genetics were not on his family's side.

You will build this hotel... You will make them all proud.

'Busy morning?' she asked.

'Have a seat,' he said, and she pulled out the chair.

'What's going on?'

'The delay in the certification is having flow-on effects.'

She nodded. 'But it shouldn't take long, should it?'

'No...but...' She was right. It was a delay, that was all. Just a slight one.

'But what if she finds something?' she asked.

'Yeah,' he admitted.

'Is that likely?'

'I don't think for a second she's going to find Odysseus' palace. But their scans showed something. Whether that's from the nineteenth century AD or the nineteenth century BC, we won't know until they dig further.'

'And if they do find something important?'

'Then we won't be able to build on the land for years. Decades, probably.'

'So, we build somewhere else.'

'Yiayia, you know there's nowhere else. Not so close to the hotel. A lot of money is tied up in this project.' He waved his hand in the direction of the site.

'You have other money.'

He did. He could use some of his own money to make up the losses. But that was a technicality only—he saw his own money also as the twins' money, the family money. He wanted to leave the family business in a better state than he found it. It was his duty.

'Besides, you know it isn't just the money. This was Theo's plan. It was Father's plan. They always wanted the family to have this connection to Paxos. And their kids as well.'

'What about your kids, *kamari mou*?'

His kids? The thought had never occurred to him. He was never going to bring girlfriends in and out of the twins' lives—he wasn't going to let them become attached to someone they might lose again.

'Lucas and Ana are my kids, Yiayia. You know that.'

'They'll be grown and flown before long, you know. Then what for you? Thirty-eight is still young.'

'They're going to need me a while yet. It'll be years before they can take over the business. Particularly with nonsense like searches for artefacts that don't exist. What would you do, Yiayia?'

'First, I wouldn't worry so much. It will all work out.'

'How?'

'You'll find a way.' She gave him a wide smile.

Her confidence was that of a loving grandmother—blind and not reassuring at all.

That evening, it was with not a small amount of trepidation that Rose climbed up the small hill from the dig to the hotel. The Aster was not obviously a hotel but looked like a collection of villas, even a small village, spread out over the crest of the hill. The single-storey buildings were painted white, with terracotta roofs. Bougainvillea bushes hung over the paved pathways and the air smelt of the oregano and mint plants that filled the garden beds.

She wandered around, looking for a reception area, and stumbled across the building he had taken her to yesterday. Alessandro was nowhere to be seen, but an elderly lady was sitting in a chair in the shade and two teenagers were sitting with her. The boy was looking at his phone and the girl was reading a book.

The twins.

They looked to be the right age. If they were the twins, she had found his home, but she needed to be at the hotel proper. She turned.

'Excuse me,' said the woman, in heavily accented but perfect English. 'Are you Miss Rose?'

She stopped. 'Yes, I was looking for Alessan… I mean, Mr Andino.'

'We call him Uncle Ali,' the girl said.

'Or Boofhead,' said the boy, and they both laughed.

The woman, presumably their grandmother, waved at them to stop and stood slowly and with effort.

Rose moved towards her. 'Don't get up; just tell me where I might find him.'

'He's out, but I'll show you your room.'

'I really don't want to impose.'

'No, not at all. We're glad you've come to stay. Come on. Your bags are here already. I am Anastasia; these are my great-grandchildren, Lucas and Ana.'

Anastasia and Ana. They must have followed the Greek tradition of naming children after their maternal grandmothers, but, sadly, there were two generations missing between these two women.

She followed them through a large wooden door and into a courtyard paved with cobblestones. A few bright-blue doors led off the courtyard.

'This is you,' Anastasia said, pushing one open and revealing a small, comfortable room. 'You have a bathroom and your own terrace. Our kitchen and living area are through there.' She pointed across the courtyard to a small garden, and a patio covered by a trellis that was in turn covered with more bougainvillea. 'Please, make yourself at home.'

'And our pool is through there, but be careful, because Lucas pees in it,' Ana said.

Lucas hit his sister. She screamed and Alessandro approached, red-faced and furious 'What's going on?'

'Nothing, Ali'

'You're yelling and punching one another in front of our guest.'

'Come, come.' Anastasia ushered the teenagers away, leaving Rose alone with Alessandro.

'I'm sorry about them. They behave most of the time.'

'It's fine, they're just kids.'

'But old enough to know better.'

His anxiousness at the twins' behaviour was strangely endearing. She wanted to reach out and reassure him by touching his arm, or wrapping her arms around him. She stepped towards him and looked into his eyes. She saw shock and surprise and pushed her arms firmly down by her side.

He led her into a bright, beautiful room. Bay windows faced out onto a garden and fresh flowers sat on table next to the king-sized bed.

'Will this be comfortable?' he asked, with a slight but still perceptible tremor in his voice. The room was lovely, but it was not exactly what she'd expected. It was not in the hotel, but a room that was part of the family home.

'This is your home, not the hotel.'

'It's attached to the hotel.'

'But this…' *It's beautiful, what are complaining about?* 'It's your home.'

She would be closer to Alessandro than he'd led her to believe. She'd hardly be able to avoid him. And how far away was his bedroom? Not that she would ask that. And, besides, she didn't know if he shared his bedroom with anyone.

'Are you worried about privacy?'

Heavens, no. She didn't need privacy beyond her own room and bathroom. This was already more luxurious than most digs. 'I've got more privacy here than at Myra's with the others.'

'Then it's my family. I am so sorry, I will speak to them.'

'No, not at all.' His grandmother seemed lovely and the kids active and precocious, as teenagers should be.

'Who else lives here?' she asked.

He considered her through narrowed eyes.

'Just me, my grandmother and the twins. Our rooms are across the courtyard, in the main building.'

Just his family and him. He did not appear to have a partner. Or children of his own.

Alessandro hadn't been sleeping his way around the world, as she'd assumed.

Strangely, the truth was painful, but in a different, bittersweet way. He hadn't left her for other women, he'd left her to be a father for these children who were not his own. He hadn't left because he was a scoundrel, he'd left her to be a good man.

And the ache that left in her chest somehow hurt more.

'Sorry, I… That is, thank you, Alessandro. It's very generous of you to let me stay.'

He nodded. 'I'll let you freshen up.' They both looked down at her loose beige trousers and white shirt, now dusty with dirt. 'And then, if you like, I would like to take you for dinner.'

CHAPTER SIX

Rose washed the dirt of the day away with a quick shower and put on a long, flowing dress that was covered in a pretty blue-and-white pattern. The colours had reminded her of Greece, so she'd packed it. When she had, she hadn't had the slightest inkling that its first outing would be on a dinner date with her old flame.

Date? No. This was not a date. It was a business matter. She was here for work and he owned the land on which she was digging.

A purely professional outing.

Hair brushed, lipstick on, she took a last look in the mirror and a deep breath before walking out of her room, uncertain where she should go to meet him.

She didn't need to worry. He was standing in the courtyard, under the bougainvillea, looking at the sky. Not at his phone or watch, but the sky.

He turned at the sound of her door clicking closed. Their eyes met and she felt it in her throat.

She wanted to be immune to these reactions, but her body had other ideas.

Alessandro wore white trousers and a blue shirt, the same cornflower-blue of her dress. He had rolled up his sleeves, exposing his smooth, tanned arms. The top two buttons of his shirt were open and his sunglasses were slipped down the neck of it. Their outfits matched as though they had planned it.

Blast. Looks like a date, walks like a date, quacks like a date.

It was only a date if they intended to kiss at the end of it. In a flash, she thought about his lips on hers, her arms around him, how his hard body would feel against hers. No, she had to be careful. She didn't really know the man who was standing before her. She didn't know what else he was hiding. He might be more honourable than she had believed, but that didn't mean she could trust him.

She was not going to kiss him. Ergo, it was not a *date*.

He walked her to a car, a convertible, and opened the passenger-side door for her. She raised an eyebrow. 'Nice car.' When they'd been students, she'd assumed he was as cash-strapped as she'd been.

'May as well enjoy the sunshine.'

She couldn't argue with that.

They drove north, away from the village, and

he explained, 'I've made a booking at a place in Gaios, but we have time for a drive around the island.'

'The whole island?'

He laughed. 'Yes, it isn't very big. You can walk most places, but Gaios is about five miles away, so I thought we'd drive.'

He drove her along winding cliff roads that took in the west coast of the island and the setting sun. They drove past beaches and another village. As the road turned at the tip of the island, he pointed across the sea.

'Corfu is over there.' He pointed and his arm crossed her body. He didn't touch her but her skin still tingled.

'Yes, I'd love to visit,' she replied.

'You've never been?'

She shook her head.

'I'll have to take you.'

'Trying to distract me from work?'

'Not at all. I'm merely trying to show you around. Besides, I'm pretty sure Odysseus spent some time there.'

'Now you're making fun of me.'

He clutched his heart. 'I would never. Besides, I'm also pretty sure he's fictional.'

'That isn't very patriotic of you.'

'While I'm pretty sure he did not exist, he is still very important to the Greeks. And to Ionians, in particular. There are some sites in Corfu there that would interest you. We have a hotel there as well, and I do often visit for work. Next time, maybe you could come with me.'

She was determined to find something on her site, but she also didn't want to pass up a chance to discover Corfu.

'We'll see,' was all she could concede.

They drove down the coast and the air blowing over the car was like balm after a day in the sun. He smiled across the console at her but, when he saw she'd seen him, he looked back quickly at the road.

It was beautiful.

He pulled over to the shoulder of the road. 'Look.' He nodded to the ocean. The sun was resting just on top of the horizon. The sky glowed yellow and orange, and the water was bathed in pink. They took a moment to watch it and take in the magnificent view.

'Down there are the blue caves. And the Tripitos Arch. We can't see them from here, only from the water. If you like, I could take you some time.'

She wanted to laugh. 'Don't you have a job? Or is your job distracting me from mine?'

'I do have a job, but I consider it my duty to show all visitors around the island.'

'Oh, you offer all your guests private tours?' Her mouth was dry as she spoke.

'Only the special ones. Hospitality is my business.'

'So, you aren't trying to distract me from my work?'

'No! I can't believe you would suggest such a thing.'

There were two possibilities, she reasoned. Either he was trying to distract her from her work, or he wanted to spend time with her. The second possibility sent a shiver up her spine, despite the warm evening air.

'Let's go,' he said, once the sun had all but disappeared and the horizon seemed to glow from below.

Rose was looking to her right, over the ocean, when the car stopped suddenly and her head hit the head rest with a thump.

'Oof.' She rubbed her head.

A brown goat stood on the road before them. Alessandro honked the horn. The goat looked at the car and she could have sworn it shrugged. Alessandro honked again, but the goat walked in a circle and then sat, resolutely, in the middle of the road. He honked again.

'Do you know the definition of insanity?'

'I'm sure you're about to tell me.'

'Doing the same thing over and over again and expecting a different result.'

He switched the engine off and pushed open the door. He walked over to the goat, waved at it and said something in Greek she didn't understand but was probably, 'Get out of the way.' The goat sat where it was. He pushed the goat's bottom with his foot but the goat just looked annoyed and didn't budge.

Rose opened her door and walked over. 'Shoo,' she said. 'Get out of the way!'

'You think it's an English-speaking goat?'

'It might be. Get off the road, off the road, shoo!' she tried again.

He laughed. 'What was that bit about insanity again?'

She gave him a wry grin.

'Okay, smarty-pants, what do we do?'

'I don't know.'

'You don't?'

'No, I don't.'

'But there are heaps of goats here.'

'And honking usually works.'

He met her eyes and they both laughed.

'We'll just have to stay here,' he said.

'Fine by me,' she replied. Because, truly, there was nowhere else in the world she'd rather be than here, in this stunning place, with Alessandro giving her a smile that was flipping her stomach and her whole world upside down.

Rose tried pushing the goat's bottom with her shoe but it just turned its head and glared at her, then let out an annoyed bleat.

'Maybe it's sick,' he said.

'We should call a vet.'

'There's no vet on the island.'

'Really?'

'There are only a couple of thousand permanent residents here.'

That explained the calm, relaxed, friendly lifestyle. Everyone acted as if they knew one another because they actually all did.

'The island is that small?'

He nodded. 'When the tourists come in summer, it seems like there are many people, but they only stay for a few weeks at a time at most. Or they just come for the day from Corfu. We don't have a vet. We depend on Corfu for a lot of our services.'

That was why the hotel was so important. It wasn't just about his own family, it was about his island family too. The hotel would be a big employer and would fill restaurants and shops besides.

Still, that was unfortunate, but finding ancient ruins was important too.

'Should we turn around? Go back?' she said.

'What if it is sick?'

Alessandro approached slowly, patted the goat's back, worked his way up to its ears and petted it like he would a dog or cat. He was tender and careful.

'And?'

'It does feel hot. And a bit out of it.'

The goat's eyes were closed slightly, but it might only have looked that way because it was happy to be petted. She imagined Alessandro rubbing the soft skin behind her ears and gulped.

'Do you think it belongs to someone? It seems happy for you to pet it.'

'Maybe, but I don't know who. Not many people live on this side of the island.'

'Are there that many domesticated goats on the island?'

He shrugged. 'Probably.'

They looked at one another and laughed. 'Goats, dogs, cats. You've seen them all.'

He was right; there were cats and dogs everywhere. They looked healthy enough, they were being fed, but they wandered from place to place as if they belonged to everyone and no one.

'I think we should get it to a vet,' he said and, even though her stomach was starting to feel hungry, she agreed.

'How?'

'I'm going to try and pick it up. Open the boot.'

'You can't be serious.'

'Do you have another suggestion?'

'Um…' No. She didn't.

'There should be a blanket in the boot.'

She went to the car, opened the small boot and found a picnic blanket.

He probably uses it for romantic picnics…

She shook the thought away. So what if he did? She would probably return to London in a few weeks and get on with her life without looking back at Alessandro or Paxos.

She passed Alessandro the blanket and he walked round the goat, looking for the best angle.

'Are you sure?' she asked, but he didn't respond.

After studying the goat a moment longer, he threw the blanket over it and grabbed it. The goat squealed but Alessandro had it. He took two steps towards the car and the goat grunted, leapt from his arms and ran off into the olive grove. The momentum of the goat's kick pushed Alessandro back and he landed bottom-down on the road.

She rushed to him and knelt. 'Are you okay?' He wasn't bleeding, but he wasn't talking either. Before she could over-think her actions, she slid her arm around his shoulders. Their faces were next to one another, only a breath away. 'Alessandro, are you hurt?' His shoulders were warm and firm beneath her palm.

His lips were parted, his breath coming fast. He looked into her eyes, pupils dilated. Was he hurt? Or was he, like her, wondering if he should move that inch closer and press his lips to hers? She licked her lips and saw his eyes glance down and notice. His chest rose and fell, and with the exhale he closed his eyes and nodded. 'I'm fine, just winded.'

She leant back, feeling disappointed and foolish. He was just winded, not thinking about kissing her at all.

'You were really worried about it, weren't you?'

He shrugged.

'Are you really okay?'

He rubbed his stomach and arm. 'I think I'll have a bruise or two tomorrow.'

She stood and held out a hand to help him up. He looked at her offered hand and studied it for a moment before he accepted it. Just like their handshake the other day.

His arm was strong and their opposing weights balanced one another out. He released her hand as soon as he was upright and steady. She stretched her fingers out, hands tingling after his touch. Alessandro brushed himself down, took a final look towards the olive grove and said, 'Let's get going.'

Gaios was clustered around a sheltered emerald bay. Brightly coloured buildings lined the waterfront and sailing boats bobbed in the calm blue water.

She had arrived in Gaios by ferry a few days earlier but had not had time to explore before catching the bus to Ninos.

She was glad to return to look around, but she wasn't about to admit that to Alessandro. He was definitely up to something. If that something included a tour of Gaios, and a dinner as good as the restaurants they passed smelt, then she'd go along with it but she was not going to be distracted from her work.

He parked and they walked along the paved streets before stopping at a waterfront restaurant. It was modern and sleek, rather than traditional and rustic. 'It has the best seafood in Paxos.'

He was probably right. She could tell just by the smell that surrounded them and the delicious-looking dishes she saw being delivered to other patrons.

Their table was next to the water, and once they were seated, Alessandro ordered a bottle of champagne.

'Is that all right?' he asked once the waiter had left.

She nodded. She'd never been able to resist champagne and was touched that he remembered.

Looks like a date, walks like a date, quacks like a date.

She breathed in and took a proper look at her surroundings. This place felt a million miles away from her real life; it was even far removed from the site she was digging on. Whatever his motivation for asking her here, there was no doubt that Alessandro had designed a perfect evening.

Apart from the goat.

'How's your arm?' she asked.

He rubbed his shoulder. 'I think I'll live.'

'I'm glad,' she replied, and before she could stop herself she smiled at him warmly.

He met her gaze and returned a smile equally as warm, eyes deep and soulful with enough gravity to pull her in and under.

No!

She dragged her gaze and thoughts away from him and picked up her menu. She thumbed its corner. 'Do you come here often?' The question was lame but it was far better than getting lost in the spell of Alessandro's dark eyes.

'I've been here a few times. The calamari is good.'

'Great, let's have that.' She shut her menu, unsure if she would be able to eat anything, given the way her stomach was twisting itself in knots.

A waiter lit the candles on their table and they sipped their champagne. Sitting across from him, Rose felt memories from their time together in Athens flooding back. She looked over the harbour and tried to push them away.

Perhaps Alessandro was thinking the same thing when he asked, 'Why do you like to dig up the past?'

This was a question she occasionally asked herself. A love of ancient history had led her to archaeology. But Alessandro's question was more abstract than that. He was asking something more fundamental—about her. When they had been together for those brief weeks in Athens, she had told him how her father had left to start a new family when she'd been seven. But she hadn't had the chance to explain to him the gnawing sense of rejection that had followed her through her childhood and teens. The knowledge that she wasn't enough. That she wasn't worthy of love.

As an adult she'd tried to rationalise his behaviour. She'd learnt to understand that people fell out of love. That people did betray their lovers. And that people could also be cowards when it came to ending relationships. That some people simply found it easier to walk away and start a new life without looking back.

But she'd never been able to understand why her father had cut her from his life so completely. The one thing she knew for sure was that she hadn't been enough to get him to stay. She hadn't been important enough for him to want to keep her in his life.

But his question wasn't about her past, it was about her work.

'To understand how we got here. To make sense of the past.' She looked at him for a long time, but not studying his features. Heaven knew they were easy to look at, but looking into his eyes was risky. 'I thought you were interested in that too.'

The smile dropped from his face.

'Maybe; I don't know. Now I don't have that luxury. These days I have to look after the future.'

His comment struck her as condescending. 'Ouch.'

'What?'

'That was a bit harsh.'

'It wasn't mean to be,'

'It sounded like you were suggesting I haven't grown up. Implied that I lack responsibility. I may not have a family, but I have responsibility. To my colleagues, for one. To my profession.'

He narrowed his eyes. 'I'm sorry, Rose, I was under the impression that you didn't want to be tied down.'

'I don't. That is, not with the usual things—mortgage, pets...'

'Boyfriend?'

Had he just asked that? Were they going down *this* conversational route?

'A good relationship shouldn't tie you down, stop you from living the life you want to live,' she said.

'And have you found that?' His tone wasn't demanding, but soft and hesitant. The question made his voice crack, and her resolve to keep her personal life or lack thereof to herself broke.

'Not at present.' She could have volunteered the fact that, since him, all her relationships had been short-lived. Commenced on the basis that she would soon be leaving to go off somewhere. It felt far too sensitive to admit that. Instead, she asked, 'And you? Are you seeing someone?'

He shook his head and her stomach swooped again.

'No. The twins have already lost enough. I've never wanted to bring someone into the twins' lives.'

She nearly spat out her drink. 'Seriously? You've been celibate since...me?'

The look he gave her made her insides warm. 'I didn't say celibate. I meant there hasn't been anyone serious, long-term.'

He hadn't been in love since her? No, he hadn't said that exactly, just that he hadn't had a serious relationship. Rose was momentarily short of breath, her chest heavy. There hadn't been anyone else since her. Her thoughts were a tangled mess, her emotions more so. On one hand, she was happy that he hadn't loved anyone since her.

Except, she reminded herself, he had. His niece and nephew. He'd left Rose for them in the past and they would be his only priority in the future. It sounded as if he had no intention of starting a serious relationship with any woman, including Rose.

Luckily their food arrived at that point and the delicious smells of the dishes placed on their table totally distracted her from worrying about how she felt about him.

'Riddle me this,' she said once the crispy, tender calamari had satiated her taste buds and the champagne taken the edge off her confusion and heartache. 'According to the Internet...'

'The Internet? That great oracle?'

'According to the Internet, the chain of hotels you own is very successful, very profitable.' *You're loaded*, she wanted to say. 'Why don't you just buy another block of land?'

He laughed. 'Suitable blocks of land don't just come up all the time. Besides, if you look around, the hotel is on the crest of the hill and overlooks the ocean. The other side is already built up and on the other side is a road. My father tried to buy this block for years. My brother also. It was always their plan and hope to extend the first Aster Hotel.'

She didn't want to say she was sure his father and brother would have understood. Because, even if his dead relatives wouldn't have minded, it was clear that Alessandro very much did. The situation was tricky and sad, but surely ancient ruins trumped the wishes of his deceased brother?

She stopped herself from opening her mouth to say as much. She considered ancient artefacts priceless, but living, breathing people were also important. As an archaeologist, her perspective of what was and wasn't important was often different from that of other people. She knew she wouldn't be on the earth for ever—only the things she did would live on.

'Building on Paxos is expensive—everything has to be shipped in. Literally. And I'll let you in on a secret. I don't own the chain, not entirely. It's split three ways, between the twins and me. I consider myself holding the business on trust for them, for until they're old enough to take it over.'

'You'd be leaving Lucas and Ana in a less advantageous position.'

'If it was just about the money, I would throw my own at it. But it isn't. It's about my father's wishes. And Theo's. It's about the legacy I pass on to the twins. The debt I owe to the village. To the island.'

'What debt?'

'When my brother died, the village rallied around. I couldn't have done it—raised them to be such happy, bright kids—were it not for them. I owe everyone this.'

'But you…you're a great businessman.'

She fancied his face turned red, but that might just have been the candlelight flickering off the table.

'Is that what Google told you?'

'Maybe.'

'Yes, I could make something else work, but not there, in the village. This extension isn't just important to the kids, it's important to everyone who lives in Ninos. Everyone on Paxos. But…'

Alessandro put down his fork and looked out at

the water. It was dark now, but the lights reflected across it. 'I have a duty to my family to do this.'

Familial duty. She only understood the absence of it.

When Rose had been twelve she'd found her father's address in her mother's beside drawer. She'd caught a bus and arrived on his doorstep, not knowing what she was going to say. The neighbourhood had been clean and still, the house much larger than the small bungalow where she'd lived with her mother. Before she could knock, she'd seen them—his other family. Two boys: five or six years old, she guessed. And his new wife, who was dark and glamorous, and had put the two boys into a flashy-looking car. Rose had run around the corner and vomited. She still saw the look of disgust on the bystanders' faces.

Duty was something directed at other people. Just like love.

'But you've raised Lucas and Ana, was that not enough?'

He screwed up his face. 'I will never fully discharge my duty to them, to my family.'

It was honourable, but didn't sound at all like the Alessandro she'd once known. The one who'd hardly ever spoken of his family. 'I don't understand.'

'When I was ten, I wanted to see how far I could swim.'

She nodded, unsure where the story was going, but let him speak.

'We were at the beach, near Ninos. I'd recently become a confident swimmer, and I wanted to test how far I could swim, so I swam out and I kept going. When I was spent, I stopped. I could hardly see the beach and hadn't left myself energy to get back.'

'Oh, no. What happened?'

'Theo. Theo found me and dragged me back. I was hardly conscious and he was wrecked. My father was furious.'

'Wasn't he worried?'

'If he was, he showed it by berating me for risking Theo's life. He yelled at me for being irresponsible.'

'That's awful.'

Alessandro shrugged. 'I was never as responsible as Theo, never as smart, never as fast. Never as good.'

'But you were younger. Much younger. Five years?'

'Eight. I don't think it mattered. Theo was just better at everything.'

Rose took a moment to digest all this. It seemed so unfair, so unjust, for a parent to favour one child over another.

That's what your father did, though, isn't it?

Rose played with the stem of her wine glass.

'And you feel a debt to Theo? That's why you want to build the hotel—because he saved you?'

'Yes, but not just for that day. For everything. For looking after me when my father died, supporting my studies. Because he's my family.'

Her heart cracked in two. He'd been carrying this guilt all this time. No wonder he was so determined to pursue this project. She couldn't tell him it was ridiculous that he felt he owed a debt to his brother, because she would have done anything to win her father's love.

'We probably won't find anything,' she said, but it was an attempt at a peace offering, and she hoped she was wrong.

He laughed. 'Then stop looking!'

'You know I can't,' she said.

He nodded. 'I know.'

They drove back in relative silence, Alessandro occasionally pointing out a sight. Rose occasionally asking what things were. He pulled up to the hotel, which was in darkness.

He walked her to her room, which was across a small courtyard from his own.

If this was a real date, this was where they would kiss.

Looks like a date, walks like a date, quacks like a date.

Her limbs were light, her lips tingling from the kiss they hadn't even shared earlier. But, no, they couldn't kiss. She couldn't let herself fall for him again.

'Thank you very much again.'

'It was a pleasure.'

She raised an eyebrow. 'Even the goat? How's your arm, by the way?'

He smiled wryly and rubbed his chest and arm. 'It'll be fine. This reminds me of our first kiss,' he said. 'Do you remember?'

His question knocked the air out of her. Of course she remembered. She didn't remember many kisses with perfect clarity—the taste, the pressure, the temperature, the look in the eyes—but that first kiss with Alessandro would always be one of them.

She could only nod. Athens... A summer evening, much like now.

'You were wearing blue, just like you are now.'

That was a detail she hadn't retained.

'You wore a black T-shirt. Your hair was...'

He lifted a hand and ruffled the neat cut he wore now, curls tamed. 'Yeah, it was a bit wilder.'

'I like the new cut.'

'You do?' The hope in his voice made her stomach swoop again. *Damn.*

'We'd been walking around the Plaka all night.'

'We'd been talking and walking for hours.'

After dinner they had explored empty streets for hours and hours, talking, laughing. It had been one of the most memorable nights of her life. It had been close to dawn when he'd walked her back to her dorm. Even there they'd stood for an hour talking before he'd finally taken her hand.

What had taken them so long? She'd known, and suspected he had too, that they would kiss—and more. She'd even believed, in those pre-dawn hours, that this was the man she with whom would spend her life. So there was no rush. No urgency.

She looked at him now, fully prepared to be pulled into his eyes and under. But the look in his eyes wasn't open and hopeful. It was hard. Closed.

'Good night, Rose,' he said without looking at her.

She expected to feel relief, but was only disappointed. Why bring up their first kiss if he was only going to close her off like that?

Suddenly, she wasn't sure if was worth digging some things up.

CHAPTER SEVEN

ALESSANDRO HADN'T SEEN Rose since they had had dinner that evening in Gaios. He'd travelled to Corfu to attend some meetings and had then flown over to Crete to visit the properties he owned there.

Back on Paxos, after checking in with the kids and his grandmother, his feet led him down the hill and to the dig. To his untrained eye, it appeared that more ground had been levelled, and a few additional trenches were evident. In the hot afternoon sun, most of the team was sitting under a grove of olive trees, sipping water and fanning themselves.

Someone had strung up a green tarpaulin between an olive tree and a post up the hill to offer some protection from the sun. He proceeded down the hill and spotted Rose under the tarp. Her white hat bobbed up and down as she scraped away intently at years of sediment, focused, determined.

Single-minded.

He knew he had to let it play out, let her search for what wasn't there. She wouldn't stop until she was satisfied there was nothing to be found. Ordinarily he'd find that sort of determination impressive. It was just a pity she was exercising it here, on his land. His family's land.

Her sweeping motions were fluid and repetitive and easily hypnotised him into a trance. He could watch her for hours, and he had—on lazy afternoons when they'd sat in the National Gardens, she reading, he pretending to. In the early hours of the morning as her chest had risen and fallen with each sweet breath.

And now.

The sound of a truck pulling up on the road behind him alerted her; she turned and looked up the hill in his direction.

Damn. Caught.

She looked at him but didn't wave. If he walked away without at least speaking to her, she'd know that his sole mission had been to spy on her. He sighed and made his way down the hill.

'Hey,' she greeted him. 'When did you get back?'

'Just this morning.'

The rest of the team stayed where they were under the trees, but fell silent and still, watching and listening.

'Come to spy?'

He needed a purpose for coming down here. Fast.

'No, I just came to see how you are.'

'I'm well. And, no, we haven't struck gold. Or bronze, for that matter.'

He smiled, supposing it was some sort of archaeology joke.

The truck that had arrived moments ago was now reversing loudly and manoeuvring itself into place.

'What's that?' she asked.

The steel: he'd forgotten it was being delivered today.

'I'm not sure,' he lied.

'It looks like it's making a big delivery.'

She wouldn't find anything here, but it did feel insensitive to be flaunting the new building in front of her.

'You know, there are other islands that may have what you're looking for.'

'I've been researching Odysseus for years. There's a lot of evidence suggesting he came here when he left Ithaca.'

'But there are plenty of other islands. Antipaxos. Kefallinia. Trust me, I'm familiar with the area. In fact, I know a special place that hasn't been explored. I could take you—show you.' His island. Well, not his exactly, but the place he and Theo had explored as kids: Erimitírio.

She narrowed her eyes. 'You just want me to waste a day.'

'No, I just want you to have the best chance of

finding something.' And taking a day away from the dig would be a bonus. As would be spending the day with her.

'I can't, I need to stay here.'

'What about tomorrow or Sunday?'

She didn't answer him but he noticed her glance over at the olive trees and her team.

'You even work on a Sunday?'

'Yes.'

'Is anyone else working Sunday?' he said a little loudly so her team would hear.

'No!' they shouted happily.

'So you'd be here all by yourself.'

'Someone has to watch it.'

'Do they? You haven't found anything, or have you?'

She clenched her jaw. If she had found something, she'd have been jubilant; she wouldn't have been able to resist telling him, rubbing it in his face.

'If there's something to be found here you and your team will find it. But what if there's something somewhere else and you miss it?'

She shook her head.

'It's a very special place. There are things left by the Venetians, but things older than that. You should let me show you.'

'Couldn't I just get a ferry?'

'Ah, no. Not to this island. No one lives on this island. It's the sort of place where, if there is treasure to be found, it has been hidden for millennia.'

Rose's eyes widened.

He had her.

'Is there any other way I can get you to stop asking me?'

He scratched his head. 'Nothing I can think of.'

'Well, okay, maybe. Thank you.'

He hid his smile the best he could.

The island didn't have any Bronze Age ruins, but it was special. It was special to him. It was where his father had taught him to sail, where he'd played and explored with Theo as a kid. He'd even once thought of asking Rose to go there with him. If Theo hadn't died, then he probably would have. They could have camped, spent a romantic night by the fire, made love on the beach.

But, as he reached the top of the hill, his smile faded. This wouldn't be like that. This trip wouldn't be to show Rose the island because he wanted to show her where he'd spent some of the happiest memories of his childhood; he was taking her there to show her a Venetian citadel and a Roman harbour. That was all.

He and Rose were still on two different paths—she had her career and he had his duty to his family. They had no more chance of a future together than they'd had fifteen years ago.

Leaving the site that evening, Rose passed the mountain of steel that had been delivered by the truck that had arrived with Alessandro that afternoon.

As if he hadn't known what they were. Heck, he probably knew exactly how many of them there were and where he planned to put them all.

Never mind, she was getting closer. The ground was getting harder, older. She could just tell. She would show him and he'd have to send those steel frames back to wherever they had come from.

When she arrived back at her room just after dusk, Ana was sitting in the courtyard and jumped up. She looked as though she had been waiting for her. It had become a habit of Ana's over the past few days, waiting for Rose to get home, stopping her for a chat. It had started with Ana asking Rose about her work, and somehow Rose's questions about what Ana liked best about school had turned into several hours of career advice. Rose didn't mind one bit; Ana was bright and interested in everything. It sounded as if she was an excellent student.

'Hi!' Ana said.

'Hello, how are you doing?'

'I'm great,' Ana said, beaming. 'Would you like to come and have dinner with us?'

'Oh, I… I don't want to intrude.' But the teenager looked so eager, Rose didn't know if—or how—she could decline. She didn't have any other plans, her body ached from crouching in the dirt all day and she didn't feel like walking back up to the village taverna tonight...

'You aren't. Yiayia said you should. Besides, I don't think Uncle Ali will be there.'

Her disappointment at that news was tinged with relief; she didn't want to spend more time with Alessandro than she absolutely had to. The desire to touch him, smell him and taste him sometimes came close to overwhelming the need to protect her heart.

'Okay, that would be lovely. Thank you.'

'Great, I'll tell the others.' Ana bounced off inside and Rose went to change.

She'd been had.

Fifteen minutes later, Rose knocked on the door to the family's main house. Ana slid the glass door open and the first thing Rose noticed was Alessandro, in the kitchen, taking a steaming dish out of the oven.

'Ali's back! Isn't that great?' Ana said, convincing neither Alessandro nor Rose that she hadn't tricked them.

'Yes, it's great,' Rose said as sincerely as she could manage. Alessandro turned but she could see the smile on his face.

They sat outside in the courtyard, under the trellis with the bougainvillea that was strung with hundreds of tiny lights. If Alessandro hadn't been there looking gorgeous and happy, then it might have been a restful evening. But every moment she spent with him was tinged with pain; either she was reminded that he didn't want her to find her ruins, or he reminded her of her youth, her heart and everything that had been lost when he'd left Athens.

'Tell me how the dig is going,' Ana said just as Rose's mouth was full.

Rose looked at Alessandro, knowing that talking about the dig in front of him was hardly the most sensitive thing to do.

Ana noticed the look they shared. 'Please just tell me. Why do you think there's something here? Tell me what you hope it will be—in your wildest dreams!'

Rose chewed her mouthful slowly and thoughtfully.

'Go ahead, please tell her,' Alessandro said.

'Oh, I hope it's a palace. Or a temple, maybe. I hope that it is something as old as the Bronze Age.'

'The Bronze Age…that was before the classical age,' Ana said to her brother, who then rolled his eyes.

'I'm not an idiot,' he said.

'Something like Pompeii?'

'Nothing as well preserved as that, given that there's been nowhere near as much volcanic activity here than in the Tyrrhenian Sea.'

'You say that like it's a bad thing,' Lucas said between mouthfuls.

'It's a very good thing for the Ionians, but it means that the chances of finding anything as well-preserved as Pompeii are not high. But that doesn't mean we won't find something of interest.'

Ana was full of questions about how they knew where to dig and how long it would take, which Rose answered politely.

Alessandro glowered, but even Lucas looked as though he was paying attention.

Once everyone had finished their meals, and when Ana took a break between questions, Rose thanked them all very much and pushed back her chair.

'Oh, and it's my birthday on Saturday.'

'And mine,' Lucas grumbled.

'Oh, I completely forgot,' Ana said to her twin brother and laughed.

Alessandro looked at the twins through narrowed eyes, and Rose could tell he was itching to tell them to be polite, but she found the bickering siblings endearing. She didn't have any siblings and, for all their arguing, she could tell they were close and loving.

'You should come to my birthday party,' Ana said.

'*Our* birthday party,' Lucas corrected.

'I'm organising the party,' Ana said.

'It's still my party.'

'Oh, yeah? What have you done for it?'

Alessandro stepped in between his niece and nephew. 'Please don't feel as though you have to come,' he said to Rose.

He didn't want her there.

'It's not just going to be kids, but other old people too,' Ana said. Alessandro buried his face in his hands and his grandmother laughed.

'Oh, I didn't mean that you're old, just that everyone from the village will be there. Please come.'

Maybe it was Alessandro's discomfort, or maybe just how earnest Ana looked, but Rose nodded. 'I'd love to come. Thank you all very much for dinner.'

'I'll walk you out,' Alessandro said.

She was about to tell him that wasn't necessary, but the other members of the Andino family exchanged complicit smiles, and she judged it was simply easier to let him. They walked together in silence back through the house and to the courtyard.

'That wasn't my idea, you know—to trick you into coming to dinner.'

'Oh, I know. That scheme had fifteen-year-old fingers all over it.'

'I'm sorry.'

'Don't be. *I'm* sorry that she wanted me to talk about my work all night. I'm sure that was just about the last thing you wanted to listen to.'

Before she knew it, they were back to where

they'd been the other night, standing in front of her door, wishing one another goodnight. It would have been better if he'd simply let her walk by herself. It was ten metres across an internal courtyard; she would have been safe.

'You don't have to come to the party—I can make up an excuse for you, if you like.'

Ahh, that was it. His real reason for coming out here.

'You don't want me to come?'

'No, I didn't mean that. I only mean that you shouldn't feel obliged to come.'

'I don't. I like Ana. And Lucas. And your grandmother.'

He lifted the corners of his lip. 'They like you too.' He stepped towards her and her body swayed to his. They held each other's gaze. One more step and they would be in each other's arms.

He shook his head. 'I'm sorry, that was wrong. But sometimes I forget myself.'

Her heart dropped. *What's really the problem?* she wanted to ask. *The twins are older now, they aren't babies. In a few years, they'll have finished school.*

But she knew the answer.

The problem, as always, was her.

She wasn't enough. She wasn't enough for him.

Rose could easily work seven days a week, particularly when a deadline was looming. She wasn't sure how serious Alessandro was about his six-week deal. If they found a trace of something before that date, she figured she would be able to get enough people from the museum or even from the village to support the work continuing.

She was more worried about the email from the museum that had dropped into her inbox that morning, notifying her that they would stop funding her at the end of the month. She wasn't so worried about herself; she had some money of her own and enough leave to stay longer if required. But her colleagues would have to leave. They were all dedicated workers, but not so dedicated that they would be happy to work for free. And most of them did, understandably, want to enjoy some of the pleasures Greece had to offer while they were here.

It was four p.m. on a Saturday afternoon and everyone, except for Gabriel and her, had already left for the taverna. They had been focusing on the site where the resistivity meters had been showing shadow. Whatever they were going to find, it would happen soon. Rose's trowel hit something hard. She scraped further and cleared more dirt.

'Look at this,' she said, but Gabriel was already over her shoulder.

'Stone,' he replied.

'Yes, but what sort? Let's clear from here.'

Gabriel knew what he was doing and the pair

of them soon had an area about a foot long uncovered. It was all the same piece of smooth rock.
And rock that had been smoothed away or cut
by someone at some stage. Her heart was racing.
This was it.

'What are we going to do?' Gabriel asked.

'Keep going?'

'Don't you have a party to get to?' he reminded
her.

It was a relief to have found whatever this was,
even though she'd never doubted there would be
something here. But it still might prove to be
nothing significant. A couple of abandoned slabs.
A statue, if they were really lucky.

'You're right.' If Rose was late to the party,
Alessandro would no doubt come looking for her.
And not for any amorous reasons, but to check
up on her.

And once he saw this? There was no need to
alert anyone to this unnecessarily when it still
might turn out to be nothing.

'So you'll leave now? Promise?' Gabriel asked.

'Yes, but please don't tell anyone just yet. Let's
wait until we're sure it's not just a rock.'

He grinned and saluted.

'See you tomorrow,' Rose said.

'No, you won't. Tomorrow's Sunday.'

'Oh.' That was right—Sunday usually followed
Saturday.

'And aren't you touring the islands?'

'Yes.' Rose sighed. And she had promised Ana she would go to her birthday party that evening as well. Two doses of Alessandro. One dose might not hurt, two in a row might prove dangerous.

'We can swap if you want to,' Gabriel teased.

She did want to…and yet, she didn't. She had to go sailing with Alessandro now or he'd really get suspicious. And she wasn't ready to tell him about what they had found that afternoon. Not just yet.

And maybe a little part of her was a bit curious about his secret island. It would probably turn out to be nothing and she could tease him about it at her leisure.

'But, hey, let's use one of the tarps to cover the ground.'

'So no one sees?'

'No, in case it rains,' she replied. Gabriel knew as well as she did that the brilliant blue skies above them were not about to release a torrent; it was best if no one got wind of the fact that they had hit their slab. When she knew more, then she would break the news to Alessandro.

Where was she?

The party was in full swing, the band was playing, people were eating and drinking. Half the village was here.

But not Rose.

Ana seemed occupied enough, chatting to her friends, but every now and then she'd look over to him and frown. He couldn't believe Rose would let his niece down.

She'll be here, he told himself. Something must have come up.

Alessandro stood near his grandmother, keeping watch over the comings and goings. Making sure he was on hand to welcome all the guests.

'Where's the lovely Rose?' Yiayia asked.

He ignored the fact that Rose was now known as 'the lovely Rose' and said, 'I don't know, but I'm sure she'll come.'

'Oh, yes, she will. She asked me what gifts she should buy for the twins.'

'She did?' He hoped she didn't feel obliged to. It was awkward enough that she had felt obliged to come to the party at all.

'Yes. Is that surprising?'

'She doesn't know them very well.' His plan to get Rose to know his family had had another effect he stupidly hadn't anticipated—that they might become attached to her.

'But she has been invited to their party—it's polite to bring a gift. I don't understand you sometimes, *kamari mou*.'

'Why not? You've known me since I was born. You understand me better than anyone.'

'Yes, even better than you understand yourself.'

'Then?'

'I don't understand why you're so strange around her.'

He was not awkward around Rose; his grand-mother was just digging for information. 'I'm not.'

'You are. You fidget.'

'I what?'

'You fidget. And sway. Like you don't know if you're going forward or backward.'

Her answer surprised him and he didn't know how to respond.

'Well, if I don't know whether I'm going forward or backward, it's because she's thrown a big spanner in my plans. In all our plans. My life is in a holding pattern until her time on the island is up.'

She laughed, 'Oh, Ali, it isn't that. You think you're focusing on the future, but you can't until you deal with the past.'

Deal with the past? He wasn't the one whose head was focused on what was lying under metres of dirt. His head wasn't caught up in ancient times.

'That's ridiculous, I don't have anything to deal with.'

'Don't you? You're different when she's around.'

'Of course I am! I'm on tenterhooks. I'm worried that the whole plan for the kids is going to be ruined. I don't understand why no one else seems to be. This was father's dream. Theo's as well. It's not nothing.' He owed it to his family.

She touched his arm gently. 'No, it isn't nothing. But you won't fail them if it can't happen.'

Alessandro crossed his arms. He didn't know how she could be so flippant about Theo. It was as though she was forgetting him. He was Lucas's and Ana's father, his brother, her other grandson. Theo had been brilliant—a gifted student, a talented sailor, a natural businessman. And a loving father. Every day Alessandro strove to be half the man that Theo had been.

He had to prove that he wasn't the irresponsible son they all thought he was.

It was about time he got himself a drink. At the very least he should stop listening to his grandmother and her theories. He should go to Rose's room, knock on her door and demand her explanation for standing up an impressionable sixteen-year-old.

Yiayia continued. 'You could never fail them. Look at how you've raised these kids.'

'I didn't do it on my own.'

'No, but I could not have done it without you. And I think you have made the bigger sacrifice.'

He didn't need to turn to know that, at that moment, she was looking across the room at Rose.

'I don't think I realised it, until now. Until I met her. I figured she was just a summer fling. But now I see otherwise,' Yiayia said.

He took a deep breath and turned to look where his grandmother was looking.

The room fell silent or maybe his heart just stopped beating. She took his breath away—literally. Her long hair was plaited and wrapped around her head like a Hellenic goddess. Her dress hung just below her bare shoulders in silken folds. He knew of no statue as perfect.

'She looks lovely, doesn't she?'

Alessandro was too distracted by Rose to lie to his grandmother. And what would've been the point? Denying that Rose looked beautiful would have been like trying to convince her that the sun wouldn't rise. 'Yes, she is.'

'Classical. That's what her beauty is. Which is fitting, don't you think?'

'Why?'

'Because her job is studying the past. But, when something is precious, it is precious for ever.'

He frowned. She didn't know him as well as she thought she did.

'What are you standing here talking to your old *yiayia* for?' She gave him a gentle shove. 'Go get her a drink.'

Arrive late, leave early. She didn't mean to be rude but she needed to keep her distance. For his sake as much as hers.

Alessandro had come over to her with a glass of wine when she'd first arrived, but had disappeared soon afterwards, leaving Rose with Anastasia and some of her friends. When her friends were chatting with one another animatedly in Greek, Anastasia turned to Rose and said, 'I understand you knew one another. Years ago. Before.'

There was no point denying it. She nodded.

'He was different, wasn't he?' the older woman said.

'Yes, he looks different now.'

'More handsome?'

Rose laughed. 'He was handsome then too. Just in a different way.'

'He's still the same man.'

'No, I don't think he is.' Rose hoped that she wasn't being rude by contradicting his grandmother, who no doubt knew him better than anyone, but he was different now. He had changed. He used to love reading and long conversations. The Alessandro of fourteen years ago would have loved her search for ancient treasure. He'd wanted to travel the world. He'd wanted to change it. Rose sensed he'd suppressed a part of himself when he'd moved back here to take over the business.

'He always had this in him. He was always loyal and dedicated.'

Once Rose would have agreed. But by showing loyalty to his family he had let her down.

'It isn't the path he would have chosen for himself, but that doesn't make it bad,' Anastasia continued.

'No.'

'He's always held a torch for you.'

Rose nearly choked on her drink. Really? She was going there? She and Alessandro had mostly avoided talking about their past as much as possible. It was as if they had both agreed it was a no-go topic. That suited them both just fine. 'What?'

Anastasia nodded. 'There's never been anyone else.'

Rose was hungry for information but the more she asked, the harder she pressed, the more she would give away, and Anastasia was clearly not one for keeping confidences.

'Me?'

'You're the woman he met in Athens?'

Was she? She had no idea he had told his grandmother about Athens. It surprised her that he had.

Rose nodded.

'He was different when he came home.'

'His brother and sister-in-law had just died; he'd just become guardian to two kids.'

Anastasia studied Rose closely and for longer than was usually considered polite. Rose tried to remain calm and unwavering under the older woman's gaze. She had nothing to hide and would stand by her comment: if Alessandro was different when he'd come home from Athens, it hadn't been due to her. He had just suffered an enormous tragedy and his life had changed for ever. Rose had been completely forgotten.

Anastasia squeezed Rose's arm and didn't say anything else. She understood, which was somehow worse. She reached for a carafe of wine on a nearby table and poured Rose another glass.

Anastasia turned to talk to one of her friends in fast Greek. Rose tried to follow the conversation for a moment then nodded and moved away. While it had been lovely of Ana to invite her, she was not going to interrupt the sixteen-year-old's evening with her friends.

And that left, of all the people she knew here, Alessandro. He was standing in a group of men, talking, and they were all watching him. She was too far away and the music was too loud to hear what he was saying, and she wasn't sure she'd be able to understand it in any event. But, even though she couldn't hear, she could understand body language and these men were all listening intently to Alessandro, deferring to him and laughing at his jokes. One of the men—who was shorter, wider and at least twenty years older—nudged Alessandro's arm and started a one-on-one conversation. Alessandro shook his head at the man, who was insisting on something.

Then to her mortification they both turned and looked in her direction. More words were exchanged between them and they began to move in her direction. Alessandro grabbed the man's arm and pulled him back, but the man shook off Alessandro's grip and approached her.

Oh, no.

As the man headed towards her, his stare was focused on her. Alessandro followed quickly behind.

'You're the archaeologist?' the man said when he reached her.

She nodded. She resisted the urge to reply, *one of them*. That would only anger him further, and she had no wish to do that. Particularly when she had no idea what she'd done to upset him in the first place.

Charm was her best defence so she offered him her hand. He looked at it as though he'd been offered a dead fish. From behind, Alessandro cleared his throat and the man accepted Rose's hand limply.

'I'm Dr Rose Taylor.'

'Demetri.'

'Pleased to meet you,' she said in Greek. Her Greek was purely conversational and she hoped their discussion would stay at that level. She already felt at enough of a disadvantage.

'Demetri is our builder,' Alessandro explained.

'Oh, I see.'

'You've delayed me. I've had to lay off my team and now I've lost them to another project.'

That was not her fault.

'I'm sorry to hear that, but it's out of my hands,' she said.

'You could just walk away. Sign the permit. Leave us to it.'

'It might look like that, but I really can't. My team know we're not done here. They'll tell the museum, the Ministry of Culture.'

Why didn't these people see that a significant archaeological find would help their island?

You're going to have to discover something pretty special. A couple of broken bricks isn't going to satisfy them.

'If you were a good boss they'd be too scared to tell anyone,' the man said, and Rose froze.

For crying out loud! This man was actually suggesting she lie to the authorities and threaten her employees. He was the limit.

'I'm not going to lie and I'm not going to threaten anyone,' she said, hoping her Greek was as firm as her tone.

The man stared at her and seemed to loom over her, even though they were the same height. She had no doubt he could flatten her with a simple shove.

Alessandro stepped around the man and put himself in between the pair of them.

'Four more weeks. I told you. Your team will be back from Ithaca by then and you can start.'

The man snorted, but at this point another man joined them, a younger version of Demetri. He took the older man's arm and said, 'What's going on, Papa?'

'He's a little frustrated about the delay,' Alessandro said.

The younger man sighed. 'We've talked about this Papa…it's just a delay; the project isn't cancelled.'

Alessandro took Rose's hand, led her away from the men and back to his grandmother. As if a tiny eighty-something-year-old woman would provide her with an appropriate shield. Though she probably would, Rose thought. No one in this room would touch Anastasia and to get to Rose they'd have to go through her.

Alessandro kept his hand on her arm. It was warm, secure. She was annoyed by how good it felt. 'I knew it was inconveniencing you. I'm sorry I didn't appreciate how much it was putting others out,' Rose said.

'Don't worry about him.'

'I… He seemed…'

'He's angry he's had to lay off some staff; he won't do anything. He's all hot air.'

'Why do you use him?'

'He's not a bad man, he's just stressed.'

Rose rolled her eyes.

'And this is a small island. If I want to use someone local—and I do—there isn't anyone else. Look, he won't bother you again.'

Rose wasn't worried the man would hurt her,

but she was worried about any feelings of ill will the islanders might harbour against her or her team. Most people had not only been friendly but welcoming and helpful. But what if the ones that weren't got to them? She didn't want to upset the locals or put them out. She truly believed that finding something would be good for Paxos.

As long as you find something good.

Alessandro squeezed her arm and lifted his hand. 'Will you be okay?'

She nodded. 'Of course.'

He turned and walked towards the band. The drummer gave a drum roll and someone yelled, 'Speech!'

The crowd gradually fell silent. Alessandro cleared his throat and began to speak.

'Thank you everyone for coming here tonight. Thank you particularly to the teenagers for putting up with the old people.'

He looked in Rose's direction and winked. Her chest warmed; no one else in the crowd understood the joke and that somehow made it even more special.

'We're here to celebrate the birthdays of these two amazing children. If you've joined us tonight, then you understand why I'm the one standing here now and not their parents.

'To Lucas and Ana—I tell you this every night, but I'm telling you again—your mother and father loved you more than life itself. I know they're watching over you from somewhere. We all miss them every day, but we are so glad that you're both in our lives. I know I could never replace your parents, but being your uncle and raising you has been the biggest privilege of my life. I love you both so very much and wish you both a very happy birthday. Please raise your glasses. Happy Birthday, Lucas and Ana!'

The crowd lifted their glasses, or at least Rose thought they did; her eyes were full and she couldn't see properly. She took a gulp of her drink and wiped the tears away.

Her vision cleared in time to allow her to watch Alessandro hug his nephew then take his niece by the hand and lead her to the dance floor. The band began to play again.

He'd left her to become a parent to these re-markable children. She couldn't resent him for that, not one little bit. The kids both adored him and, seeing them tonight, getting to know them over the past few weeks, she knew that he had done a remarkable job providing a happy, safe and loving home for them.

The thought soothed her.

Yes, circumstances had meant she hadn't en-joyed the life with Alessandro that she'd once hoped for, but who was to say they would have lasted the distance anyway?

Lost in her thoughts, Rose didn't realise that Alessandro and Ana had danced their way in her direction. Ana grabbed Rose's hand and pulled her out with them. The song was fast and the three of them danced with one another for a minute or so until the song changed. With more confidence than Rose could have mustered as a sixteen-year-old, Ana picked up Alessandro's hand and placed it in Rose's. Then, to make sure, she nudged them together.

'You two have to dance,' she said.

Rose couldn't refuse a birthday wish, but she looked at Alessandro. 'You don't have to, if you don't want to.'

'What if I want to?' He slid his arms around her and she did the same. She felt warm, secure, safe. They swayed together, though she was careful to leave an inch between them. Their arms might be holding each other's but they didn't need to press their bodies against one another's. She had to maintain her self-control somehow.

Even with a breath of air between their bodies his arms still embraced her waist, warm and secure. Her arms were draped around him and she could feel his strong shoulders beneath the thin fabric of his shirt. The urge to slip her hands under the shirt was almost overpowering...

Small talk! That was the solution.

'It's a great party.'

'We do it every year.'

'That's lovely.' Despite her best attempts, she still couldn't steady her heart rate.

'I like to make a fuss.' He paused, cast his eyes down and explained, 'It stops me feeling guilty.'

He was unable to meet her eyes but she studied him. The guilt he felt about his brother was crushing him. 'You have nothing to feel guilty about. You've done an amazing job with these kids,' she said.

'I'm not done, though, am I? I still have to keep building the family business to pass on to them.'

No wonder he was so determined to build this hotel; it was about guilt. Not just about his father, but about Theo too. And, no matter how misplaced or misguided it was, guilt could be a powerful force.

'Is money what they really need?'

'No, but they need their family legacy. And it's more important for them to have it because their parents aren't here.'

Oh, she wanted to sigh. These kids knew they were loved. But, equally, nothing could really compensate for an absent parent. The pain she felt from her father's abandonment had never left her. But it was different with these kids—their parents had been taken from them. Rose's father just hadn't loved her.

Then, as if someone had whispered them a special request, the band struck the opening bars to a familiar song. But Ana was nowhere near the band, and besides, no one else could have known the significance of this song.

In Alessandro's embrace, breathing in his scent, Rose was already reminiscing about Athens. When the music began, she was transported back there.

'Songs, smells…they are like a time machine, aren't they?' Oh, no, had she said that out loud?

'Do you ever think about Athens?' he asked.

In the past week, she'd done nothing else. She'd thought about their walks, their conversations, leaning towards one another over small, rickety, candlelit tables.

And also this—dancing. Bodies pressed against one another, swaying, moving against one another. Sharing the same space, the same air, the same breath.

His embrace tightened and she longed to lean into it. Surrender to it.

But, no, there was no point; that would only make the next few weeks harder.

'I remember,' he prompted, whispering into her ear, his breath sliding down her neck like a kiss.

The silent agreement they'd had not to revisit the past was now close to being ripped up. Ground into the dust.

No.

They had to focus on something else.

But what? If they couldn't talk about the past, they could only talk about the future. She was desperate to say something about what she had found that afternoon, the stone, but he was the last person she could tell.

What had happened to him? The Alessandro she had known in Athens would have been overjoyed by such news. He would have been deeply interested, would have theorised with her about what it could be.

Tragedy… That was what had happened to him. She'd never had a sibling, so couldn't say how hard it would hit her, but his brother's death had altered Alessandro.

Before she could stop herself, she pressed her face into his strong shoulder. Hugging him, being this close to him, was fraught with risk, but it wasn't as risky as looking him in the eye. He smelt of soap and jasmine. She could smell him for ever.

His arms tightened around her. They had danced to this song in Athens. They had held each other in bed while this song had played. She had played this song over and over to herself when he'd left. She had cried herself to sleep singing this song. And now he was holding her again. Her mind and body couldn't reconcile it.

And then the song ended and the spell was broken. The next song was new, unrecognisable, and it jolted her back to the present. They both pulled back at the same moment, but somehow her hand ended up wrapped in his and he lead her away from the dance floor without looking at her.

'I'm sorry,' she said.

He looked perplexed. 'What for?'

'Your brother and sister-in-law. It changed you.'

He shook his head. 'I'm still the same person, aren't I?'

'You used to believe in mythology and lost treasure,' she said sadly.

They were standing too close to the band. He looked around the courtyard, took her hand and led her to a nearby doorway and away from the party.

Once they had rounded a corner, he dropped her hand. She flexed her fingers, her skin still tingling from his touch.

'I didn't mean to be rude. It's just a shame, that's all.'

'Losing precious people makes you think differently about the past. My focus is now the future.'

The future. Always irreconcilable with the past.

She looked away from him and surveyed her surroundings.

The hotel was on one side of the hill, facing south. The view from the other side, where her dig was, faced north. She was very familiar with that view, but this one was new. From here, she could see south down the coast. The lights from the other settlements twinkled in a festive string.

'It's beautiful, I've never seen the island from this angle.'

'I should have shown you the other night when we went to dinner.'

She shook her head. 'You've been a wonderful host. Thank you again for being so hospitable, so welcoming.'

He tilted his head to one side. 'Why wouldn't I be?'

'I don't know. I guess I figured...'

I figured you didn't want to see me again.

He lifted his hand to her upper arm again and turned her gently to face him. 'What is it?'

'When you left, I thought it must have been because of me.'

'I thought I explained, I left because of my brother, because of the kids.'

'Yes, you did. But it's hard to shake that feeling of rejection. I spent fourteen years believing you'd left because of me.'

People often leave because of me.

'Oh, I see.' He drew in a deep breath and expelled it just as forcefully.

She'd said it, loud and clear. *You rejected me. You broke my heart into a million tiny pieces that no one has ever been able to put back together again.*

She had to back track. Quickly. 'I'm okay. I'm fine, but it hurt. A lot. And even though you've explained, well, it still hurts.'

Why shouldn't he know how much he'd hurt her? She continued, 'It hurt a lot. I felt rejected. I felt betrayed. And confused. So confused. I know you did it because you wanted to save me, but...

I didn't have that knowledge or perspective until just the other week.'

'I'm sorry.' He looked down, vulnerable, apologetic. 'I didn't know what else to do. I didn't want your life to be turned upside down like mine was.'

'Didn't I matter?' She could hardly speak without her voice cracking.

He pulled her back to him. For the second time that night, he turned her to face him, looked up and faced her, and her stomach swooped.

'No, I did not get over you quickly. Not at all. But you, I figured... Rose, you're remarkable, beautiful, exceptional. I figured it was only a matter of time before you moved on. Before someone came along to take your mind off me.'

It sounded like a compliment but maybe he didn't understand the insult buried within it.

'Rose, when I was young I didn't appreciate my family. I took them for granted. But then my father died, and then Theo. And when he passed away I swore to make up for it all. I didn't want my obligations to ruin your life'

'You really think that's an excuse for leaving me?'

'Yes, I do. I owe this debt, not you.'

'Debt?' she asked.

'To my family. I'm sorry if you don't understand...'

Rose turned away. *You don't have a father, how*

could you possibly understand? That was what he was saying. Maybe he was right.

Now they were talking about it openly, it was as though they were tearing the wound apart. She'd thought that cut had healed over with barely visible scars, but it was now as fresh as it had been when it was new.

'I'm so sorry I hurt you. It won't change anything, or make you feel better, but the truth is I longed for you. Sometimes it hurt so much I couldn't breathe. Or move,' he said.

She turned back to him. 'Same,' she admitted.

He pulled her into his chest and wrapped his arms around her. She buried her face in his chest and surrendered to the feeling. Wrapped in his arms like this felt so…right.

The other night he'd said that there had been no one else special in his life. But that was because he didn't want to hurt the twins by bringing someone else that they might lose into their lives. To save them heart ache. He'd said nothing about his own heart.

Knowing about his own pain didn't give her any comfort at all, but if she'd known he had a reason for leaving it would have helped her. It would have saved her all those years of not knowing. All the hours spent wondering. And it might have helped her move on.

It wasn't that she hadn't moved on; she'd seen other men. But there'd always been some part of her that she'd held back. She'd always been the first to run.

Now she couldn't run. Her feet were stuck here as if they were in concrete. She had to face him. She had to deal with him for the next few weeks, at least.

He's always held a torch for you.

Alessandro still held her close and she slowly became aware that his fingers were sliding through her hair. She felt her chest rise and fall with his. Oh, to say here, just like this, for ever.

But they couldn't. They had to move on, move forward. She lifted her face from his chest, not sure what she would see, but surprised to see him looking intently down at her. As if he'd been waiting for her to be ready.

Was she? She wouldn't know until whatever was about to happen happened. She held his gaze as his lids lowered. Her eyelids followed automatically. His lips brushed against hers. Then pulled back. A taste? A test?

A test she suddenly wanted to pass.

Her body tingled, long-forgotten sensations stirring. He looked into her eyes. The sparkle in the deep-brown depths of his eyes told her that, far from being dragged under, she would be safe. She pressed her lips back to his.

Oh, yes.

This wasn't the past and it wasn't the future. It was now. Only now, and here, with the smell of the ocean, the sounds of the party behind them and the crashing waves in front.

It was her lips as they were now, his body as it was today, older but strong, his kisses more tender yet more hesitant, sweeter. Her body fizzed and ached. The longing she felt for him was about to tip over into something she'd be incapable of stopping.

A shriek from the party made her pull back. The shriek was followed by laughter that shook her firmly back into reality.

The kiss was an aberration; that was all it could be.

'Can we…?' He shot her his most handsome smile, so suggestive she felt her knees slipping. He tugged her to him. The instant before she fell inexorably back into his arms, she extracted her hand from his.

'No.'

'But…'

'Alessandro, I don't think we should torture one another.'

He laughed. 'I think our definitions of torture are very different. If that kiss was torture for you, I apologise. I thought my kisses were adequate. I can assure you, yours are wonderful.'

He'd always been able to disarm her with his smile, to knock the breath out of her and tilt her world on its axis.

'The kiss would not be torture, but what follows would be—saying goodbye.'

'We don't have to say goodbye just yet.'

'But we would in a few weeks. Or do you want me to extend my work here?' She tilted her head; her question was cheeky, but she held her breath for his answer.

The grin he returned was wry and sad at the same time. He shook his head. 'That was unfair.'

Now he was throwing fairness into the mix. Nothing about this situation was fair.

She stepped away from him. She should go back to her room and draw a line under the kiss, but the tie to him was hard to sever. She walked to the end of the patio, the wall that overlooked the sea. Drawing in a deep breath, she tried to centre herself. This was the Ionian Sea. A place that had fascinated her for years. The myths had given her hope and comfort almost all her life.

'Alessandro, the problem is you don't want me to succeed.'

'I do, but…'

'You either do or you don't.'

'Do you want me to abandon my father's dream? My brother's dream?'

'No, but you're asking me to abandon mine. I've dreamt of making a big discovery since I was a child. I can't let my dream go either.'

This wasn't like their previous arguments, which had been combative and tense. This conversation was simply sad. Yet again, their lives were on opposing paths.

'I don't know what to do, Alessandro. I can't give this excavation up. Apart from the fact that I want to know if anything is here, signing off the permit now and walking away would be professional suicide. My reputation would be ruined.'

'I know you can't, and believe me, I'm not asking you to. I don't know what to do either.'

'Then what do we do?' He couldn't think she was happy about this situation. She wanted to return to the warmth of his arms as much as he wanted to have her. 'How do we fix this?'

'I'm not sure it can be fixed.' Was he talking about the dig and the hotel or them? 'I need to stay in Greece and look after the family business, at least until the twins are ready to take it over. Your life is wherever the next big discovery is going to be.'

He wanted to stay and build his business, prove his loyalty to his father and family. Her life was where her job took her. It almost didn't matter what she did or didn't find, the same thing that had kept them apart fourteen years ago still lay between them.

'I love it here, but I can't stay.'

'I understand. And it's too soon for me to hand the business to the children. I don't know when that would be.'

Rose suspected that Alessandro's attachment

to the business was so strong he'd never be able
to let go of it. His need to prove his loyalty was
so powerful.

He looked out over the sea as well. The evening breeze was picking up and ruffled his hair.
Her arms shivered. He slipped one arm around
her and pulled her close. The gesture was more
platonic and practical, but she leant into it just
the same. Together they watched the dark water
swirling beneath them.

'Then what?'

'We wait and see. If there's something there,
I'm sure you will find it.'

'And if there isn't anything?'

'Then…?'

'It's fate, isn't it?' he said.

'Fate?' A surprisingly romantic word for the
man who seemed to have given up on love and
happy endings.

'If you were meant to find something, it was
decided thousands of years ago. If I was meant
to build the hotel, then that was also determined
years ago. Our fates were sealed in the Age of
Heroes.'

She pondered this for a moment then laughed.
'Yes, I suppose so.'

The thought was terrifying…and freeing at the
same time.

Whatever would be would be. In the meantime, if she could just keep her distance from

Alessandro, protect her heart, then everything would be all right.

She faked a yawn and pulled her body away from his. 'It's getting late.'

'Yes, and we have a big day tomorrow.'

The sailing trip. A whole day in Alessandro's company. One part pleasure, two parts pain.

CHAPTER EIGHT

THE NEXT MORNING Alessandro readied the things he'd need for the day ahead and tried to keep his emotions in check. Angelina had put together a picnic basket for them and he was gathering a bag of things for the boat.

'It's a beautiful day,' Yiayia said when she walked into the kitchen. She eyed his casual shorts and T-shirt. 'What are you up to?'

'I'm taking Rose sailing.'

She tried to hide her smile, without much success.

He couldn't shake last night's events from his mind. The kiss still thrummed in his veins. His lips remembered it every time he opened them to speak. Each time he closed his eyes, Rose flashed beneath his lids.

But it was the conversation afterwards that was going around his head in a never-ending loop. He carried the bags out to his car. The day was already warm and humid. It would be much cooler on the water.

You don't want me to succeed.

Perhaps, but he didn't want her to fail either. What he wanted, what he really wanted, was to take her in his arms, sweep her up and take her to his bed. That was what he wanted more than anything.

He paused, hand in the air, before he brought the boot lid down on the car.

He wanted her.

Life had stopped being about what he wanted years ago. What he wanted was irrelevant. He'd buried his wishes and desires successfully up until now and it hadn't been a problem.

It wasn't a problem because the children, your family, the business, were always the most important. No other woman you ever met was like Rose.

But now Rose was back in his life—even for a short time—and he wanted her in his arms.

She was standing outside her room, shifting from one foot to the other, when he walked out.

'Hi,' she said. She wore a loose pink sundress that fell to her knees and a big straw hat. She looked edible. He imagined brushing his thumb along the soft skin of her bare arms. He shook the thought away.

'Do you have a swimsuit?'

'Will I need one?'

'Better to be prepared. Of course, if you want to go without…'

Her face turned beetroot. 'I'll go get it.'

He had to push these thoughts of Rose away just as he had over a decade ago. But this was different from fourteen years ago. Last time she had been remote; the kids had been small and had needed him night and day. He'd been exhausted with grief.

Now she was here, near him. His grief had dulled and the two children who had once needed him so much were now, mid-morning, still fast asleep. Maybe, like Yiayia had suggested, there was time for him? Maybe he didn't have to put the kids first?

Except… Rose still had her work. He still had the family business to run. At least for the foreseeable future they were unlikely to be able to be in the same country for any length of time. Which was why it was imperative he kept guarding his heart.

Rose's dig being on his land was an almost laughable coincidence, as though the gods were laughing at his expense. What had been the chances of her turning up on Paxos, on his land?

If it was odds he wanted to bet on, what were the chances of her actually finding anything on his land? Slim to non-existent.

But if she was right, and there were Bronze Age ruins to find in the Ionian, then might she find them somewhere else on Paxos or somewhere else nearby? It was no good just showing her the village, he had to show her the island. His island—Erimitírio.

Taking her there might help her understand him, his family and the connection he felt to them. The debt he owed them, even if his heart half-broke to go there. Even if was one of the places in the world where he felt closest to Theo and their father. A place that bought so many memories flooding back. If there was anywhere near by that was ancient, brimming with history, it was the island.

It was the place where his father had taught them both to sail, the place where he had taken them all for adventures, where they'd pretended to be explorers, warriors.

He hadn't been for years, not since the kids had been younger. They'd preferred to see their friends or play video games. If he'd been their real father, maybe it would have been different. But he wasn't Theo and, as much as he loved them, he always knew he was never quite enough.

Rose re-emerged from her room, glowing. His throat went dry. He was fooling himself if he thought he'd be able to keep his distance from her today. But he had to try. 'Lead on,' she said as she closed the door behind her.

Alessandro drove them down to the port at Gaios and led her out along the marina, where the sailing boats were lined up in a proud row. They proceeded to a boat he appeared to be very familiar with, stepping onto it as though he was simply crossing his threshold.

Once on the boat, he turned back and offered her his hand. She accepted and stepped onto the boat but, as she lifted her second foot and transferred her weight to the first, the unsteadiness of the boat and the water surprised her and she fell forward, almost landing on top of him, saved only by his quick thinking and strong arms.

The sensations from the night before returned: warmth; security; excitement.

'Are you all right?' he asked once she was steadied. 'Did you slip?'

'No, I'm just not very familiar with yachts.'

He grinned like a professor sensing a foolish student. 'Well, for starters, this is a sailing boat.'

That sounded a lot less solid than a yacht. It was also smaller. It was only as long as a couple of cars, had a small cabin and one tall mast. And Alessandro knew exactly how to drive or sail it—whatever the correct terminology was. She supposed she could bother to learn but that would give him a little bit too much satisfaction. And right now, with the muscles in his arms rippling as he pulled on some ropes and wound a winch to lift the sail, a slight breeze ruffling his hair, he looked pretty satisfied with himself.

And why wouldn't he? He looked as if he'd just

stepped out of a commercial for a luxury watch or some space-age razor.

'I'm sorry, I'm no help. I don't know anything about sailing,' she said, sitting back and admiring the beautiful view of Gaios port and the turquoise sea beyond…not the man on the boat.

'Don't worry, I could sail her blindfolded.'

'Please don't.'

Alessandro twisted the rope around something, secured it in place then jumped down onto the deck beside her.

'You're not worried, are you?' he asked.

Any time in the past she'd been on a vessel this small, her stomach had not been happy about it. But, if pressed, the thing that worried her most was simply spending more time in close quarters with Alessandro.

'No, not worried.'

'Ah, queasy, then?'

She winced. 'Sometimes, maybe.'

He laughed. 'This is Greece! You can't get seasick.'

'I'm sure some Greeks get seasick,' she retorted.

He shook his head. 'No, I don't think so. It would be most unpatriotic.'

'I don't believe that for a second.'

He rummaged in a cavity near the front of the boat and then tossed her a plastic sick bag. 'Just in case,' he said.

She didn't know whether to be mortified or grateful.

'So that's why you didn't want to come today is it?' he asked.

She hadn't wanted to come because she had work to be doing. A stone to be uncovered. She hadn't wanted to come because every moment she was alone with Alessandro was both wonderful and awful. But she'd let him believe it was seasickness.

'Stand up here with me.' He was at the helm behind a large wheel. 'Look out at the water and enjoy your personal tour of the islands.'

She walked towards him, still getting accustomed to the way the boat shifted under her.

'If you're looking straight ahead, the less likely it is you'll feel seasick.' He held his hand out to her again to encourage her to join him. She lifted her hand to his, knowing even before the skin touched it would be risky. As his large, warm hand circled hers, she was sorry to be right. Sparks spread from her fingers through her hand. How she wanted him to slide his hand up her arm and envelop more than just her hand…

She snatched her tingling fingers away and held onto a bar at the front of the boat, looking steadfastly ahead at the sights they were passing.

As they sailed out of the port, they passed through a channel bounded on one side by Gaios and the other by a green, lush island. 'That's

Agios Nikolaos, with the historic monastery. Built by the Venetians. You might even see parts of the walls of the observatory.' He pointed.

As they left the calmness of the harbour and entered the open water, Alessandro switched off the motor that had propelled them out of the port and began adjusting the sails.

'Now you might feel best if you're sitting here. The wind will pick up as we start to move.'

And it did. Alessandro manipulated the sails and the boat began to slice through the water. The breeze did make her feel good and, as long as she was focused outside the boat and on the scenery, she felt fine.

It was not a hardship. The view from the boat was spectacular. Green olive trees covered the slopes that wound gently down to the glistening emerald waters. They passed numerous secluded coves and bays. 'Most of these can only be reached by boat,' he explained.

They sailed up the coast in the direction of Ninos and another island came into view. He turned the boat towards it. When he changed direction, the sails no longer caught the wind and the boat slowed.

'And this is Erimitírio. It means "home of the hermit". It's been uninhabited for centuries. There's no jetty or marina, so tourists don't come. But I think you might find it interesting.'

She agreed. It was small but beautiful. She

could make out the hint of a white pebbled beach, but otherwise the island rose steeply out of the water into a rocky peek.

Uninhabited was good; unexplored was better. Myth said that, when Odysseus had left Ithaca for the final time, he'd travelled to a smaller island, where he had died. Paxos was smaller than Ithaca. But this island was smaller still. Maybe Alessandro wasn't trying to interrupt her work after all, but giving her the chance to be the one to explore this place.

Once the dig was finished near the hotel, there'd be no reason for Alessandro to keep helping her. No reason for the museum to keep funding her. If she wanted to find anything proving the legend of Odysseus, she would have to do it on her own.

'Tell me about it.'

'This is the island where Dad took us to learn to sail. Over there is the bay where my brother and I would come with a little dinghy and explore.'

'On your own?'

'Of course.'

'And do Lucas and Ana come here too?'

His smile was sad. 'We used to come here all the time together, but now they're older...' He ended the sentence with a shrug.

There was such weight and sadness in that shrug. She'd thought he might be relieved now the twins were older, but no. He had clearly loved sharing their childhood with them. The feelings of pride he'd spoken of last night were mixed with feelings of nostalgia and happy memories of their childhood.

'But speaking of Odysseus…' He changed the subject.

'Which we weren't.'

'Speaking of Odysseus, they say he was nearly shipwrecked here.'

'Let's face it, most Greek islands make that claim,' she said.

He smiled. 'No, but this was real,' he said jokingly.

He was teasing her and she nudged him playfully. When he looked down at her, his eyes were serious and she felt her body falling towards him.

No.

It was just the waves, the boat bobbing gently on the sparkling water. She had to keep her distance. Last night had taught her several lessons. First: Alessandro's kisses tasted even better than they had fourteen years ago. Second, how little self-control she had when alone in his company.

'Seriously, apart from Odysseus, the Romans came here. They built a fort.'

'Really?'

'Truly, but that fort was mostly demolished by the Venetians to build their own. It's called the Citadel. But traces of the Romans still remain.

I'm sure if someone had appropriate qualifications they could study the area and write about the history of it.'

'I'm sure they could. And, maybe once that person has found the Bronze Age ruins on your land, they could turn their attention here.'

He raised an eyebrow but she couldn't make out his expression—doubting...or worried.

'Why is it called the Island of the Hermit?'

'Because of the hermit.'

'So I assumed.'

'It was centuries ago. Maybe millennia. He was a stranger from across the seas and came to live on the island.'

'Is there fresh water there? What did he eat?'

'That's a good question, and no. There's no fresh water.'

'So how did he survive?'

'Every week, a man called Leonidas would take him some fresh fruit, bread and water. The hermit paid in gold coins. Apart from that, he lived on fish.'

'He must have really wanted some peace and quiet.'

Alessandro grinned. 'And Leonidas kept bringing him his supplies and he kept paying for them. Eventually, Leonidas died, so his son took over. But eventually his son died and *his* son took over, and then his.'

'And so on?'

'And so on. For over three hundred years the hermit kept paying them.'

'That sounds suspiciously like myth, Alessandro.'

'Of course.'

'I thought you didn't believe in myths and legends.'

'I don't believe in digging up my land for them. That doesn't mean I can't tell the stories. I'm Greek. Of course I tell these stories.'

He said it with a pride that was infectious. But for once it wasn't ancient history she wanted to know about, it was Alessandro's.

'How often would you come here with your father and brother?'

'Whenever my father had time.'

'Was that a lot?'

'He made time. Like I've tried to do.'

A lump formed in Rose's throat and expanded to block it. Alessandro had been such a devoted father to these children, maybe even more devoted since they were not his natural children. Why were some men like that, and yet others couldn't even be bothered to look after their own? Like her own father.

Because he didn't love you. You weren't enough.

Her mother had tried to tell her that he'd left *her*, not Rose. But he had left Rose—he could have asked to see her. He could have contacted her. He could have returned her calls. But he never had.

Her mother's words bounced off her, unheard, because he had abandoned Rose every bit as much as her mother. Because, when it came down to it, she wasn't enough. He loved his new family more.

Alessandro had a habit of being able to read her mind at moments like this. 'Tell me about your family.'

'There's nothing much to tell. My father left when I was young, my mother worked hard to support us both. It wasn't bad. But she did not teach me to sail around a Greek island.'

'Your father, yes, I'm sorry. You did tell me about him. Has he ever...?'

She shook her head. 'No, he never contacted me. A couple of years ago my mother heard that he had died.'

'I'm so sorry.'

'It's fine. I hadn't seen him since I was seven.'

It wasn't fine, but she didn't want to speak about it.

Her father had been dead for six months before her mother had found out. She'd passed the news on gently, but it had still stunned Rose. Now there was no hope of a reconciliation, no hope of an explanation.

To avoid discussing her own family, she said,

'Your family's much more interesting. You never told me much about them, you know.'

'We weren't together very long,' he replied.

No, they hadn't been. She looked away from him and over the water, into the distance.

'I'm sorry, that came out wrong. I didn't mean to down-play what we had. I only meant that I didn't have time.'

'I know.' She nodded. 'We talked about a lot of things in those weeks. Our hopes, dreams, plans for the future. You just told me your family was from the Ionian Islands. And, now I'm here, I see how incredibly important they are to you. I'm also sorry because I didn't think to ask.'

He reached over, took her hand and squeezed it. 'Don't apologise. I don't think I realised how important they were to me until they were gone. I was a selfish young idiot.'

She touched his arm, 'Don't say that.'

'It's true. I took them for granted. Until it was too late.'

'And, besides, I was just a summer fling,' she said.

He turned to face her and gave her his full attention. His gaze held her and her stomach swooped, even before he spoke. 'Just to be clear—I never thought we were just a summer fling. I wanted to spend my life with you.'

CHAPTER NINE

HIS DECLARATION STUNNED her speechless. Once upon a time him telling her he'd wanted to spend his life with her would have made her heart sing, now his words just squeezed her heart with pain. They reminded her of a life she'd never lead.

'I think I hoped the same,' she admitted. 'For a few weeks.'

His mouth dropped and something like pain gathered behind his eyes.

Fourteen years ago she would have grabbed a declaration like that with both hands. Now, it just made her wistful for what might have been.

'You were going to travel the world searching for history and I was going to follow you writing about the present. It was going to be an amazing life,' he said.

She couldn't help but smile. 'It would've been wonderful.' And, because something she didn't want Alessandro to see was brewing inside her, she quickly added, 'But we've both still done amazing things. You've grown a hotel empire, raised two kids.'

She needed him to know that those things were important too. Most of all, she needed to believe it herself. There was no point dwelling on what he had just said; it had been a comment about the past, that was all. It certainly wasn't what he currently felt.

Without telling her what he was doing, Alessandro manoeuvred the yacht closer to the island.

'What are we doing?' Her skin was warm, maybe from the sun. Or perhaps because of what Alessandro had just confessed and the conflicting feelings thrashing around inside her.

'Now, we've got some choices here. We can sail around to the other side of the island where there's a better beach to bring in the boat. Or I can leave her here. It's only about fifty metres; do you think you can swim?'

She'd swum fifty metres many times before; she could make it. She studied the shore, the narrow white beach glistening between the turquoise water and the deep green of the island. Most importantly, the water looked cold enough to cool her down.

'Or we can just stay here, but I thought you might like to explore,' he prompted.

'Swim, I guess,' she said. 'Last one in's a rotten egg.' She kicked off her flip flops and dived into the sparkling water, dress and all.

The coldness of the water shocked her at first but after a few strokes her body adjusted. Once away from the boat, she stopped, treaded water and looked back up. He was on the boat shaking his head. She turned and made even strokes through the water. The salt water felt amazing on her skin.

After a while she stopped and turned to make sure he was actually following her. He was now in the water and following behind her. Before she knew it, the sandy sea bed appeared beneath her and she could touch the bottom. Now she was here on the island, she wished she'd brought a towel somehow.

Shortly afterwards Alessandro also emerged from the sea, salt water dripping from his bare torso. Her mouth went dry and her body instantly felt warm again. His chest was broad and his stomach as taut as it had been all those years ago. A memory of trailing her fingers across his naked skin crept annoyingly into her mind and her muscles clenched. Heaven help her.

He shook something from his back.

'What's that?' she asked.

'A dry bag,' he said, unzipping it. He took out two towels and two pairs of sand shoes.

He handed a pair to her. 'You'll need these; we're going for a walk.'

'Where to?'

'You're full of questions, aren't you?'

'But of course. I want to know where we're going.'

He laughed again. 'Just come with me and see. The island's only a hundred metres across, so it won't take long.'

With mixed feelings, she watched Alessandro pull a T-shirt over his head. They made their way across the small beach and into the scrub beyond. He led her to a narrow, mostly overgrown, path that led up the hill. Alessandro had been here many times because he knew exactly where to find the path. While the island wasn't currently inhabited, it might have been at one point.

'Are you going to show me where the hermit lived? Or is he still here?'

'Ha-ha-ha.'

She followed him in silence after that, concentrating on not slipping on the almost non-existent path. It was a long time since it had been regularly used.

They rounded a bend and she sucked in a deep breath. 'Gorgeous.'

He turned back to her and grinned. 'Isn't it?'

Before them, close to the summit of the island, was a pile of ruins. It had clearly once been a small building. A temple, maybe. A castle. It was hard to say.

'Is this the hermitage?'

'Unlikely. This was a citadel, built first by the Romans, restored by the Venetians. Come and see.'

He couldn't have stopped her rushing over and stepping over the first stones to get a better look.

'Yes, it's not ancient. At least, not that I can see. The foundations might be...but, oh, look!' After she'd stepped over what had probably once been the threshold, she could see that part of the building was still intact. Four walls and part of a wooden roof remained. The rest was covered by a tree that had grown in the corner, making the space half-ruin, half-treehouse. 'It's lovely.'

She was suddenly aware that he was watching her, not the ruins. Watching as she leapt from place to place, exclaiming to no one in particular what she saw. His gaze was a heavy weight on her heart. It was full of admiration, but also loss. It simply reminded her of what could never be.

I never thought we were just a summer fling. I wanted to spend my life with you.

What a thing to confess. And now—now when there was no hope of them having a life together. The stolen kiss they had shared last night had even been too much of a risk. If she wasn't vigilant, the carefully constructed wall she had built around her heart to protect it from falling for Alessandro again would start to crumble. Just like the ancient fortress she was standing in now.

'It's mediaeval,' she said, running her fingertip along some etchings on the wall, a long-faded painting. 'When did you say it was built?'

The pink dress she wore over her swimsuit was slowly drying, though her red swimsuit was still visible through the thin fabric, which clung to her curves, leaving little to his overactive imagination. *Beautiful.* She was standing in front of him like an untouchable goddess, a sea nymph. Turned out bringing her here and encouraging her to jump into the sea hadn't been the smartest idea he'd ever had.

'This was built by the Venetians in the thirteenth century. But they weren't the only ones who lived here. The Ionian Islands have been occupied by everyone from the Romans to the Ottomans to the Italians.'

He had a feeling he'd already told her this. And it was something she was bound to know herself, but right now he was clinging to small talk to keep himself focused on something other than the thin dress clinging to her gorgeous body.

She turned and gave him a Mona Lisa smile. He had no idea what she was thinking.

Once upon a time he'd known exactly what was going on in her brilliant mind. Now, she was giving nothing away. Including how she felt about what he had confessed to her on the boat.

I wanted to spend my life with you.

She was right to treat his statement lightly; it didn't matter what he'd wanted all those years ago. Right now their wishes and dreams were completely opposed to one another's. He wanted a hotel, she wanted to dig up his land.

Rose walked around the ruins, stroking the walls.

I wish she were looking at me the same way she's looking at these ruins.

'Has anyone ever done a proper survey of this place?'

'I have.'

She turned and grinned. 'While I'm sure you did a great job, I meant a professional.'

'Ah, no. Would you like to?' He knew this would just remind her of the job she was meant to be doing, but he suggested it anyway.

She rolled her eyes.

He held up his hands in surrender. 'Seriously, it's all here—you'd hardly have to dig and you'd be sure to find something.'

'It isn't my era.'

'But it could be. Honestly, I thought you should see this place.'

The smile on her face was wide and dreamy. 'It is amazing. Thank you for bringing me here. I would love to have more of a look around.' She sighed.

'Feel free.'

He'd forgotten what being with Rose was like. It had been a conscious decision to push his memories of her down deep and to throw away the key. Watching her now, he remembered why. If he'd remembered this for the past decade, he would've lost his mind by now. He wouldn't have had the resolve to do what he had to do for the twins.

Now that he remembered, now that the knowledge of her touch, the sensation of her kisses, was at the forefront of his mind, what would he do? He didn't know how he could move on. He only knew he couldn't go back.

You don't know if you're going forward or backwards.

'It's gorgeous. Oh, Alessandro.'

He wanted to believe she was talking as much about him as the island.

'Look how the vines have nearly swallowed it. I think they're the only things holding the stones up in some places.'

He remembered coming here as a kid and experiencing the same sense of wonder as she was now. This had been some back yard for him to explore. He'd probably taken it for granted, but not many kids got to sail to their own private island and pretend they were pirates or kings or warriors.

'It goes on for ages!' she exclaimed. She must have noticed the ruins that led down to the other side of the island and the small harbour.

'Are you hungry?' he yelled out to her. 'There's some lunch on the yacht.'

She didn't reply and he shook his head. She was immersed in the ruins and would be for ages.

He watched her walk away. She disappeared over the ridge and he thought he would go to her in a moment. But in the meantime he decided to go back to the boat and get some water and a hat for Rose. The day was a little cloudy, but he knew her skin was sensitive to the bright Greek sun.

He set off back down the hill. He hadn't been here for a while, but his feet remembered the path well, each rise, fall and corner. Once he emerged from the scrub onto the narrow beach, he saw the colour of the sky was different on this side of the island—grey, close and cold.

Damn. It looked as though a storm would be here within the hour. The boat was exposed where it was now; he should have brought it in to the cove to begin with. They might be stuck here for some time. His phone was on the boat and he should get that to check the forecast.

He strode straight into the water. When it was deep enough, he dived in and then with long, even strokes made his way out to the boat.

Rose walked through the ruins of the citadel and out the other side. The view of the other side made her draw in a sharp breath. This side of the island dropped away, steep and rocky, down to a sandy, sheltered cove surrounded in green.

They'd probably once had three-hundred-and-sixty-degree views of the sea from the top of the fortress. No wonder they'd built it where they had.

'Where did this hermit of yours live, then?' she called out to Alessandro. There was no answer. She thought he'd followed her, but clearly not. She'd become carried away, exploring. The place was amazing. It wasn't her usual bag; the small fortress had been built some time in the Middle Ages. It was in ruins, not half-buried like the things she usually looked at. But it was magical.

And the connection to Alessandro made it even more special. She scrambled back over the ridge of the hill to the citadel and called out again for Alessandro.

No answer.

The bag with the towels was lying where he'd left it. She picked it up and followed the path back the way they had come, expecting to see him around each corner, past each tree. She didn't expect to see him in the water, swimming back to the boat.

Surely he wasn't leaving her here? *No, he wouldn't leave you.*

He did once.

She stood and watched, mouth open, as he made his way through the water with bold, strong strokes. He reached the boat and pulled himself up onto it. She waved. He didn't wave back.

He just hasn't seen you.

'Alessandro!' she yelled as loudly as she could but still he didn't turn.

He just hadn't heard.

Or he's pretending not to.

In the distance it looked as though he was winching up the anchor. She waved again, yelled. The wind blew her hair back off her face. The wind wasn't on her side, either. Alessandro went to the controls. Water churned at the back of the boat and it began to move.

He's really leaving.

He's leaving me here.

The wind wasn't only stronger but cooler than it had been when, foolishly, she'd dived into the water. Back towards Paxos, clouds were gathering on the other side of that island. The clouds were moving at quite a pace and rain would come in the next few hours.

She watched, frozen on the spot, as the boat moved from where it was anchored around the tip of the island and out of sight. Back south, in the direction of Gaios.

It was one thing to leave her in a bar in Athens without an explanation. It was quite another to leave her on a tiny island in the middle of the Ionian Sea with rain coming. She paced back and forth to expel the excess adrenaline that was currently flying through her veins.

She walked back up to the fortress, scrambling to the highest point to get a better view of the water and see if she could still catch a glimpse of Alessandro and his boat. But even the best vantage point, one that let her see all the way back down the coast to Gaios, didn't afford her a glimpse of him. It was as if the boat had just disappeared. He'd been in that much of a hurry to get away.

The others would realise she hadn't come back with him. How would he explain the fact that she was no longer with him? How would he explain her disappearance to her team, to his own grandmother? There must be some explanation for what he was doing. But what?

What if it took another fourteen years before she found out what was his reason for leaving her stranded on this rocky outpost? What if, like with her father, she never really found out why?

The wind became colder and the dark clouds closer. The speed at which the storm came upon her was remarkable.

Maybe he's just getting help.

Then why wouldn't he tell you? Or why not just get you to sail with him?

It made no sense.

If it was going to start raining, she needed to find some shelter. The citadel was in ruins but the tress that had inundated it might provide some shelter. She clambered over the rocks back up to it. She took herself into the furthest corner under the stones and green canopy, sat, wrapped her arms around her knees and tried to breathe.

CHAPTER TEN

SHE DIDN'T KNOW how much later it was that she heard someone call her name.

It sounded like Alessandro, but he was probably back on Paxos by now.

'Rose! Rose, where are you?'

Alessandro was running through the ruins of the citadel before she could get up. Before she could hide the feelings that were painted across her face.

'What are you doing?' he asked.

'It's about to start raining I didn't know where else to go.'

'Yes, I'm sorry about that. We're going to have to stay.'

'Stay?'

'I brought the boat around to the cove down there. It's more sheltered and we can bring it right up to the beach. Though the walk up this side is much steeper. I also got some things.' He held up two bags. 'But we shouldn't stay here. I know a better place.' He turned and made his way back out.

Rose still didn't move. Her body was still weak with fear, still processing what was happening.

He hadn't left.

Noticing she wasn't following, Alessandro turned back. 'Rose, what's the matter? Are you all right?'

The feelings churned through her, just like the waves in the ocean.

He wasn't going to leave you. He was bringing the boat in, fetching things.

'Rose?' This time he dropped the bags and knelt down to her. 'It's just a storm. We could sail in it, but we don't have to. We can just wait it out here.'

She forced herself to get up, despite the weakness in her legs, the confusion in her heart. She didn't want to have to explain her reaction to him.

'It'll be fine. It's not a big storm, but given your queasy stomach I thought we should ride it out here.'

Far from leaving her, he was suggesting they stay here to save her from getting seasick.

It didn't make him a bad person—in fact he was a very good person—but she still hurt. Her limbs were still weak.

Why had her mind instantly jumped to the worst possible conclusion?

It was a perfectly natural reaction, considering he's left you once before. Considering he has no intention of building a life with you. Considering people leave you.

He would leave her at some point. Maybe he wouldn't abandon her on an island in the middle of the sea. But once she found treasure on the land he wanted for his hotel?

He might care for her, and those feelings might even be strong, but when decision time came, when it came to the crunch, he was going to choose his family and his island over her. He'd said as much last night. He needed to stay in Greece to look after the family business; her life was wherever her work took her.

'Did you think I'd left you?' he asked.

'Of course not.' She attempted a laugh, but it came out weak, almost teary.

'Then what's the matter? What happened?'

She felt a small drop of rain on her face. He looked at the sky.

'Tell me,' he said.

'I watched you lift the anchor and move the boat. You disappeared without a word. What did you think I'd think?'

'First, you were so absorbed in looking at the ruins I didn't think you'd notice. And then, if you had noticed, I guess I thought you'd see the storm and figure it out.'

'I did see the storm.'

He pressed lips together. 'You thought I'd leave you in a storm? Alone?'

'No, I mean…' *Yes. Yes, I did.* 'You left me once before.'

'Hey, I thought we'd talked about that.' He picked up her hand. Conflicted feelings crashed inside her—embarrassment, relief, anger. But also pleasure at the way her hand felt as he turned it over in his and studied it.

'We did talk about it, and it's silly. But I couldn't help it.'

More drops of rain hit her face and the wind whipped her hair around her face.

'Come with me.'

'Where?'

'You'll see.'

He stood and offered her his hand again. 'Trust me. Please.'

Her hand was heavy at her side and it took more strength than she seemed to have to lift it.

He's asking you to follow him, he's not asking you to hand over your life. You can do this.

She lifted her hand to his. He helped her up.

It was so easy for him to ask for her trust, so much harder for her to give it. She knew now why he'd left her in Athens, but he'd still kept the real reason from her for fourteen years. He'd thought he knew what was best for her. She couldn't trust him with her heart again.

He led her, hand still in hers, along a path that lead down the other side of the hill. She shivered. She'd come dressed for a warm day but had foolishly jumped into the sea fully clothed to cool her mind and body from thoughts of Alessandro.

Now she was under-dressed and over-exposed. She hoped wherever they were going was warm.

She was hoping for a large tree, maybe an overhanging rock. She hadn't allowed herself to hope for this.

'It's a cave.'

'It is.'

'How big?'

'Big enough, but we're lucky the storm is coming from the west. We can light a fire without smoking the place out.'

Alessandro placed two large bags on the ground next to her. 'Do you want a fire first or something to eat?'

'You have food?'

'Of course. What sort of tour guide do you think I am? Food or fire?'

She shivered.

'Fire it is. Why don't you unpack the bags?'

As Alessandro gathered some wood and created some magic with it near the entry to the cave, Rose looked through the two bags he'd placed at her feet, a sports bag and a cool bag. She unzipped the sports bag and found a picnic blanket, a couple of towels and two large sweaters.

'Were you a boy scout in a former life?'

'In this one.' He grinned back at her from the fire that was beginning to smoulder.

She unzipped the cool bag and exclaimed, 'Ah! Food!'

Food, wine and everything besides. She pulled out bread, cheese, dips, grapes and olives. Once the fire was lit, he joined her on the blanket and twisted open the top of the bottle of wine.

She passed him two of the plastic cups she found in the bag. Their fingers brushed and her hands tingled.

The red wine warmed her, as did the fire, and the bread filled the empty space in her stomach. The memory of the horrible moments when she had believed she was stuck on the island began to fade. She began to take in her surroundings more closely. Firelight flicked off the cave walls. It was a natural cave, but humans had made their mark.

The world had shrunk to just the two of them. His hair was still damp, scraped off his high forehead. She could look at him all day.

'What is this place? Is this where the hermit lived?'

'Given that I don't actually believe the story about the hermit, probably not. But I do think there are worse places to get stuck.'

'Were you trying to get us both stranded?' The thought of being here, alone with Alessandro, and not having to think about the rest of the world for a time was not unappealing.

'Of course I wasn't trying to get us stranded. I know you. I'm not powerful enough to bring a storm. You'd need a god for that.'

Her very own Greek god.

She had a vague recollection of describing him that way in her diary. Before he'd left her in Athens, of course. His hair was drying in the heat from the fire and flopped into his eyes. She wanted to brush it back, run her fingers through it. She wanted to touch him freely and openly, as she once had. She took a big gulp of wine instead.

Alessandro stood up. 'Wait here just a moment.' He turned and then added, 'I'm not going far.'

She scooted forward to the cave's entrance, far enough to remain out of the rain but so she could see the instant he returned.

This was silly. She was a grown woman—she never worried about being left alone. She travelled the world by herself, for crying out loud. This island was hardly the middle of nowhere. Someone would have found her if she'd failed to return to Paxos.

Alessandro wouldn't leave you.

Maybe not alone on a deserted island, but she had no doubt that one day, somewhere, he eventually would.

When he returned to the cave moments later with some more firewood, Rose was sitting at the entrance to the cave, looking out expectantly.

His chest constricted.

He had really scared her. How could she possibly believe that he'd leave her here?

You left her once before. And her father did too. You haven't given her a reason to trust you. You kept things from her, made decisions that affected her without talking to her. You let her down.

Next time he'd tell her where he was going. If there was a next time.

He put the armful of firewood down in the cave where it would have a chance to dry before they needed it. If he had possessed the power to summon a storm, he would have used it to do much more besides. He would have used his power to bring his father and brother back—or stop them dying in the first place. And he would have used his powers to keep Rose by his side.

But he wasn't a god. He was just a man. And sometimes not a very good one. Today was a prime example.

He'd managed to forget to check the forecast and had got them both stuck on the island. That was something neither his father nor brother would ever have been foolish enough to do.

Worst of all, he'd managed to scare Rose in the process, and put her in danger, because he'd just been thinking about himself. He was kidding himself if he thought he was as responsible as his brother.

He sat back down on the blanket.

'The rain's settling in, I'm afraid.' He touched his hair. It was wet. Rose passed him a towel.

He should have thought more about how his sudden disappearance might have affected her, but he was being honest when he'd said he'd thought leaving without an explanation had been the right thing to do. But he realised now she'd never understood he'd done it for her. Theo's death had turned her life upside down as well, but she hadn't even known.

He poked the fire. It flashed brighter, like the feeling in his gut.

Guilt…that was the sour sensation in his throat and gut. He'd underestimated the depth of her feelings for him.

If she loved you even a fraction of the way you loved her, then she must have gone through hell…

'I'm sorry again.'

'I know,' she replied.

'You didn't even let me tell you what I'm sorry for.'

'I know you're sorry for leaving me. Both times.'

But had she forgiven him? Even if she thought she had, her reaction to him leaving to move the boat just now showed that he'd affected her deeply. He didn't know how he'd do it, but he had to fix it.

And, since he couldn't come up with any other plan, he poured them both another glass of wine.

'Tell me what it was like,' she said. 'When the kids were little. Was it very hard?'

He drew in a deep, soulful breath. If she wanted to change the subject, who was he to argue? 'Yes, it was hard, and heart-breaking. They were old enough to know that their parents were not there, too young to understand what had happened. The heartbreak was visceral; the tears, the cries for their mama and papa, tore me apart.'

He wasn't looking for sympathy, he wasn't the one who needed it, but Rose placed her hand on his all the same. It felt warm and safe. 'That must have been so hard.'

'Thank goodness Yiayia and I had each other. And everyone from the village too. We didn't cook for months. We didn't clean for months. Everyone rallied round.'

'But after a while the twins bonded with me. Properly. We'd talk about their parents, show them photos and videos. And—I think I've said this before—it was awful, but it's also been a privilege.'

'You said that in your beautiful speech last night. More than one handkerchief was taken out.'

He shook his head. 'I don't feel proud, Rose.'

'But you should.'

'No, looking after the kids was a privilege. I'm not the one who made the biggest sacrifice.'

He stared into her eyes as he said this. The firelight flickered over them, giving her a half-incomplete vision of his face. She didn't understand exactly what he meant and something, an invisible hand, held her back from asking.

She sipped her wine and felt warm. She could hear the rain pattering down outside, but in the cave they were warm. It was only mid-afternoon, yet in the cave, in the storm, it was as dark as early evening.

The fire was not only warm but comforting. An open fire had always inspired conversation since ancient times. She felt the same, in the semi-darkness and, because they weren't going anywhere immediately, the conversation flowed.

'How far does the cave go back?'

'I'm not exactly sure. Theo and I only went as far as we could with torches. He once talked about getting professionals in, but I don't think he ever did. It was one more thing he didn't get around to doing.'

Theo had been older than Alessandro, but must have been no more than thirty when he'd died. A life not even half lived.

'But we did once find some things left behind from the war.'

'Really? What?' she asked, thinking it might be guns, ammunition...a diary.

'Rubbish mostly.'

She laughed. 'That actually sounds about right.'

'Empty tins, wine bottles—also empty.'

He talked to her about the Second World War

and how it had impacted the islands. He talked of modern Ionian history too.

'You always did enjoy modern history and politics.' She moved closer to him.

'I still do. Unlike you.'

She shrugged. 'I'm not uninterested.'

'What time would you go back to?' he asked. 'If you had a time machine.'

'Oh, I love this question.'

'I thought you might.'

'It depends on whether I'm dropping in for a visit or having to live there. It would depend on whether I was a man or a woman. Rich or poor.'

Alessandro smiled at her and for a moment she stopped breathing. She adored this man like no other. 'It sounds like you may have already given this some thought. Okay, if you were going back for one day, to see one moment in time. You don't have to live there or put up with the food, the smells, the sexism or complete lack of medical care.'

It was just like being in Athens—sitting at their table in the taverna, drinking coffee all night and talking about everything under the sun.

'Then, oh…perhaps Cleopatra's death? Or maybe the Ides of March 44 BC. Or maybe…'

Alessandro laughed heartily.

'It's difficult to choose! What about you? Where and when would you go?'

He fell silent and looked thoughtfully at his

empty wine cup. He spun it between his two hands. 'To the night before I got the phone call about Theo.'

Now she did stop breathing.

'And I'd call him up and tell him not to drive that day. And, if he did, I'd at least hang around the next day and make sure to speak to you.'

Her eyes stung…probably just from the smoke. 'We can't go back.' It was a pointless, empty thing to say but all she could think of.

'I know.'

The devastation in his voice was apparent, not just at losing his brother but having his life turned upside down. Putting his own dreams on hold.

Rose's heart thudded in her chest.

'But I'd be kinder, more understanding. I know I can't change the past, but I promise to do things differently in the future. I promise to talk to you, tell you everything.'

He was talking as though they did have a future together. But, after everything they'd said, how could that be?

'Has it been awful?'

'It's been hard, but there have been good moments. But losing you…' He stopped and turned to face her properly. He picked up her hand, a gesture he'd made several times over the past day. One which still made her heart leap each time.

Rose instinctively moved closer to him so they were sitting almost shoulder to shoulder. And, because no words had been invented that could express everything she wanted to tell him, she leant forward and pressed her lips to his.

He stilled for long enough for her to freeze. For time to stop. For their lives to hang suspended between them.

Then his mouth yielded, his arms enveloped her and time sped up. Their tongues met, their lips matched each other's and her hands reached for him, making up for all that lost time.

He tasted of wine and longing, and the world spun around her.

His hand slid over her shoulder and under the strap of her swimsuit. She wanted to lie down and pull him on top of her. She wanted all of him. Now.

No.

She gently pulled her lips away from his and took a deep breath of Alessandro-free air before she was lost completely.

They both caught their breath, but she held his shoulders, and his arms were still wrapped warmly around her waist.

I don't want to let go, but I don't trust myself to fall.

'We never had a goodbye kiss,' he said. 'Maybe if we had, it wouldn't be so hard. I'm so sorry I left without saying a word and I don't know how to make it right.'

He cradled her chin in his palm and stroked

her cheekbone with his thumb. The desire to lean into him was almost overwhelming.

'I know you had a good reason to leave. It just maybe wouldn't have hurt as much if I'd known at the time.'

He nodded as he pulled her to him. Instinctively he lay down, pulling her against him, and her head came to rest on his chest, her legs around his. They lay against one another, watching the fire, waiting.

'It's actually very Homeric,' she said after a while.

'What do you mean?'

'Shipwrecks, storms. One of the reasons it took Odysseus twenty years to get home to Ithaca was because he kept running into storms.'

Safe against his chest, she felt Alessandro chuckle. He slipped his body out from under hers and turned to look at her, supporting his head with his bent arm, and she mirrored the gesture.

'Just like us, always running into shipwrecks and obstacles,' he said.

'You're worth waiting for.' She leant in and kissed him again.

The sense of contentment and completeness he felt lying here with Rose in his arms was at odds with the sensations of nervousness and excitement brewing inside him. He was complete, yet burning with want at the same time.

You can't go back but you don't know how to go forward.

He slid his fingers into her hair and his skin shivered at the sensation of her sweet breath on his skin.

'I feel we have unfinished business,' she said. 'Is that strange?'

'Not strange at all,' he said. Her words resonated through him. They definitely had unfinished business. He having left so suddenly, with so much left unsaid between them.

His stroked her cheek and neck with his free hand, curious to see if she would push him away, but she leant into the gesture. Her eyes closed slightly. He loved doing this to her. Loved seeing her body react to his touch.

With her eyes still closed, she murmured, 'I want you.'

His breath came out in a rush. 'Thank God, I want you too.' He brushed his lips against hers. Her curves lay along his and he marvelled at how perfectly their bodies came together.

He trailed kisses down her neck and then found soft pink skin behind her ear and kissed it. She shivered.

'Are you cold?'

'Not at all. That was a different kind of shiver.'

'I'm glad to hear it.' He kissed her neck again, eliciting the same physical response. He pulled her tighter. It had been a long time since he'd been with someone he cared about the way he cared about Rose. He took his time. They had all night, after all.

'I didn't bring you here to seduce you.'

She pulled back and shot him a devastating smile.

'I'd hope not. I'd hope at least you would have taken me somewhere with a proper bed. But, speaking of which, how unprepared exactly are you?'

He looked around for his backpack, rummaged and retrieved his wallet, which contained a foil packet.

He'd been with other women, but not like this. It hadn't been like this since he and Rose had last been together.

Physically they had both learnt a trick or five but emotionally, mentally, it was as though he was twenty-four again. It was old but new, fresh. They didn't break eye contact as he stroked her or when they fully came together.

The intensity shook him inside and out. He saw her.

And she saw him. All of him.

They moved together instinctively. She was soft and sensuous beneath him, but he felt raw and ragged, trembling. He took care. They took their time and he held her tight as she broke again and again with each stroke until they could shatter no further.

* * *

He hadn't meant for that to happen. He'd wanted it to, but knew it would complicate the already complicated mess they found themselves in.

He'd been right all along: with Rose a clean break was best. What had just happened between them had reignited feelings and desires he'd carefully suppressed and locked away when he'd left her in Athens. She was in a dreamy, dozy state beside him, but he was wide awake. His body might be spent but his mind was racing in every direction, at a hundred miles an hour. Everything had changed.

Or had it?

Another summer fling. That was all it could be because in a few weeks, or even less, everything would change again. She would return to her life and leave him to get on with his.

Suddenly it felt as though the walls of the cave were closing in on him. The smoke from the fire, which hadn't bothered him ten minutes ago, was now suffocating.

He had to get out.

He unwrapped himself from Rose as carefully as he could but she pulled him tighter and sighed. His ribcage started to crush his heart.

'I'll be back. I won't be long.'

She opened her eyes and fear flickered across them. 'Where are you going?'

'Just to the boat to get some things we might need before it gets too dark.'

Her grip on him loosened and he rolled away from her. He pulled on his shorts and a shirt. Rose's eyes were closed again. He bent down to give her a soft kiss and whispered, 'I won't be long.'

She'd honestly believed that he had left her earlier. That he had got back on the boat and sailed away. He'd made her feel that way. The shame was made even more suffocating because her fear was not entirely irrational.

He did want to run from her.

But not for the reasons she thought. Not because he could treat her feelings lightly. Not because he didn't care. But because he cared too much.

He'd never felt so close to her than he had in the last few hours. He'd coped with losing Rose last time by ignoring it. By devoting himself to the twins, giving them every ounce of energy and love he had. And then giving everything that he had left to the business. He'd made himself too busy, too distracted, simply too exhausted.

It wasn't healthy—he'd never claimed it was—but it had worked. Except now? Now the kids didn't need him as much. And now Rose knew the truth about why he'd left. They'd crossed a line and he didn't know how he could go back to how things were.

You can't go back, but you can't go forward.

Out of the cave, the fresh air was a relief. It was raining steadily. If had just been him, and if there'd been a little more light, he might have attempted the trip back to the main island. But Rose didn't handle waves and the light had almost faded entirely. The best thing to do would be to make themselves as comfortable as possible in the cave and stay for the night.

He got everything from the boat that would make sleeping here more comfortable—a tarp, two old blankets and some windcheaters kept in the boat for just a situation like this. The ground was level, though hard, but with this extra padding and their body heat…

Rose was sitting up when he returned. She was dressed and warming herself next to the fire. Her auburn hair spilled around her shoulders, catching the firelight. She had been keeping a lookout.

'It's still raining,' he said.

'Yes, I can see.'

He dropped the supplies he'd brought from the boat and added more wood to the fire.

'I've let them know where we are. I'm so sorry.'

'What for?'

'I don't think we should sail back tonight. And I'm not sure how comfortable it's going to be to sleep here. I've got some more things, but it's not going to be as comfortable as my accommodation usually is.'

She smiled up at him and fire spread through him in a whoosh.

'But it is very eco-friendly. I mean, the carbon footprint of this place is nearly neutral.'

He sat back down next to her. 'Well, the wood we're burning counts, I suppose, but I built this place for next to nothing.'

She moved in close to him and slipped her arm around him. 'And you know the most carbon-neutral way of keeping warm?'

She was going to break him entirely. If he spent the night in her arms, he'd lose his heart for ever.

Without meaning to, his body stiffened.

She recoiled slightly and he heard her murmur a soft, 'Oh.'

'Are you sorry it happened?' she asked and he felt her hold her breath while she waited for his answer. And he took a long while considering it. He'd loved every moment of their love-making. But he was terrified of what it meant for the future. Her words from the other night, the ones he had dismissed, now rang true all around him.

We'd only be torturing one another.

Finally, honestly, he answered. 'No. Not at all. I think it complicates things, though.'

'It does.'

'I thought we were saying goodbye.'

'It felt a little more like a hello.' Her voice was soft.

She was right. He'd been a fool to kid himself

that making love would help them resolve anything; it had only made everything more difficult.
Now the memory of holding Rose wasn't old and
distant but her scent was still in his lungs, her
taste on his lips. And it was driving him crazy.
His heart thrummed with need, his body with
want.

'Do you think you can sleep?' he asked. There
was little chance he would; his mind and body
were too awake, too alive. But it had been a long
day and Rose had to work tomorrow.

He did too, for that matter.

'I'm not sure, but I think we should try.'

He located the tarp and laid it out on the floor
to try to give a little more insulation from the
cold ground. Then he looked at the blankets—
two old blankets, the picnic rug and some towels.
He wasn't sure how to arrange them.

'You know, we would be warmer if we put
them together.'

'It's summer, we won't freeze,' he said without thinking.

Her face fell.

'I didn't mean… Oh, Rose, I just don't want
to put any pressure on you. You should join me
if you're comfortable.'

In the firelight he could see her shoulders tense.
Could see hesitation. Half an hour ago they had
been naked, holding on another. Now they were

both skittish, pulling back, neither sure where they stood. He'd really messed things up.

'With our clothes on. We'll be warmer that way,' he said. He couldn't stand the thought of her shivering through the night. It was summer, but the air was fresh in the storm. It would get cool overnight. And he needed her to know she was safe, secure, that he wasn't going to leave. And he'd hold her platonically all night to show her that.

How could she have believed he would up and leave her on an uninhabited island? What sort of monster did she think he was?

'It'll be warmer, I promise.'

Was she hesitating because he was only offering her a chaste hug, fully clothed? Or was she reluctant to get close to him at all?

CHAPTER ELEVEN

SHE SHUFFLED AWAY from him. It was clear he thought that making love had been a mistake.

'Do you want some more wine? Something else to eat?'

She nodded and he retrieved the basket and poured them both another glass.

She couldn't meet his eye as he passed it to her, afraid of the pain he'd see in hers. It hurt more than she'd been prepared for: Alessandro loving her one moment, pushing her away the next. They had just made love and now he wanted to lie on the other side of the cave.

He knows you should both keep your distance, and you know it too.

Far from resolving their unfinished business, making love to Alessandro had reminded her of everything they had lost—the playfulness, the way he touched her like no other and could read her body and her emotions. She'd never been more in tune with another person.

Sucking the olives away from the pits was at

least distracting. Before long a pile of pits had built up in her palm and she studied them, for no other reason than avoiding Alessandro's eyes.

He regretted it. He'd said he didn't but after they had made love everything had changed. Instead of growing closer, he'd somehow become more distant.

He couldn't wait to get out of the cave immediately afterwards.

If you weren't on an island he would have hot-footed it away as fast as he could. He probably contemplated swimming back to the main island.

If only she could sail, she could be the one to leave. Now it looked as though she was going to be the one abandoned yet again.

'I understand it was just a one-off,' she said.

He stilled. That was what he wanted, wasn't it? They both knew it was for the best. She had no intention of letting this man break her heart a second time and last night they had discussed why a relationship between them was impossible.

'I'm not expecting a repeat performance. I can't have another summer romance with you. And we both know that's all it can be. Some people can have no-strings affairs but I'm not one of them.'

'It's for the best,' he replied, looking at the ground and not at her.

She sat on the tarp and towels. He'd fashioned his bag into a makeshift pillow and pushed it towards her.

He lay down first on his back and patted the

ground next to him. The desire to lie next to him was only a fraction greater than the need to walk out of the cave. She lay down next to him, but facing away, and adjusted the bag that was to be her pillow. The ground was firm, but not uncomfortable. She felt Alessandro move behind her and wrap his arms around her. She might be warm, but every muscle in her body was on alert. His body felt tense pressed against hers. She willed the wine, the fire and the exhaustion from the day to overwhelm her. But it didn't.

Behind her he shuffled to get comfortable and every movement raised fresh desire that was quickly replaced by heartache. He was right: it probably would have been better if they had slept separately, instead of like this: together, apart.

'I'm so sorry, Rose.' His warm breath brushed across the top of her head.

'I've told you, it's fine.'

'Not about this. But about leaving the island earlier without telling you. I'm sorry that you thought I'd abandoned you.'

'That was my issue, not yours. I'm okay now… just embarrassed. I thought I was better adjusted.'

If there was any man who should get blame for her insecurities, it was her father, not Alessandro.

Alessandro was not going to leave her again, he was not going to break her heart, because she would be the one to leave first.

Just as soon as she got off this blasted island.

* * *

It was mid-morning the following day by the time she was showered, dressed and back at the dig. Gabriel had obviously briefed the team before her arrival and they all looked up at her, smiling but calm. They were scraping away the soil from the top of the slab to reveal its full extent. Others were already working at removing the soil from the sides of it.

'Hey, boss,' Gabriel said to her. 'Everything okay?'

Rose nodded. 'Just an unscheduled stop on a deserted island.'

His eyes opened wide. 'See anything good?'

Rose swallowed hard. 'There are the ruins of a Venetian fort, possibly built on the foundations of a Roman one.'

'Wow! No wonder you stayed.'

Gabriel didn't know the half of it.

Rose and Alessandro had left the island just after sunrise. The water had been calm, the wind light, and they'd been mostly silent on the trip back to Gaios and the drive home. She wasn't sure about him, but she had a lot to think about, digest.

They'd agreed they didn't regret making love but, from the awkwardness afterwards, it was clear to both of them it was a one-off. Last night in the cave had proven it. They had lain together, fully clothed, under the blankets on the makeshift bed. Nothing had happened between them, except a night of wondering, ruminating and very little sleep on her behalf. *He's lying here to keep you warm*, she told herself. *He's being chivalrous; you can't turn around and pull his clothes off.*

She was right: they shouldn't make love again; they shouldn't continue to play with one another's feelings and pretend they somehow had a future together.

He didn't want a relationship; he'd been very clear about that. His life was here, hers was wherever the next important dig was.

Besides, they would never agree on her search and the hotel. His dreams of development and expansion might always clash with her desire to protect the past.

Finding a trace of Homer's world in the Ionian Sea had been her dream for as long as she could remember. Building this hotel was his. It wasn't only about building a future for the kids, it was a thank you to the village that had saved his grandmother and him. They had shared his grief and rallied around in the darkest hour. Most of all, it was his way of honouring his father and brother.

She did feel a little guilty about her role in preventing him from achieving his dream, but what she wanted was important too. It sometimes seemed there were no safe conversation topics; the gulf between them arose even when she least expected it.

The problem was, making love to him didn't feel like a goodbye. It didn't feel as though any business was resolved. She only wanted to do it all again and again. She never wanted to leave him. She could, she decided, have stayed on Erimitírio for ever. Just like the hermit, she wanted to live on the island with Alessandro for hundreds of years.

So they couldn't be together again. She sighed as she picked up her trowel. No matter what, her business with Alessandro would never feel finished.

As he suspected, the team was all still there, focussing their energies on a small patch of land.

She approached him with a grin on her face, fanning herself with her hat.

She was happy to see him. She wasn't furious about yesterday, about their overnight stay or what had happened on the island. His heart leapt in his chest and his insides glowed.

'Good evening,' he replied happily.

'It is, isn't it?'

'I wasn't sure what kind of mood you'd be in this evening,' he confessed. 'I've come to ask if you want to have a meal with proper tables and chairs.' It was a nod to their impromptu meal the day before. And because he still felt bad about getting them stuck on the island.

She looked puzzled, shook her head quickly

and said, 'Oh, maybe. Come and see what we've found.'

His heart landed with a disappointed thud.

Rose moved back towards the others but he stayed where he was. She wasn't happy to see him—she was delighted to have dug something up.

She waved for him to come.

His feet moved as though moving through water and he was afraid of what he was going to see. He was relieved only to see a glimpse of stone about a metre or so long.

'Isn't it great?' she enthused.

'Um…what is it?'

'Some sort of wall, we think.'

'How can you tell?'

'It's smooth, it's been carved. It was placed here deliberately. And there's another one there.' She pointed to the side. He could only see dirt. 'They have been placed at right angles.'

He'd have to take her word for it. 'Why is it significant?'

'Because if it's just a wall, or a fence, then it's unlikely to have right angles. Only structures holding something tend to have right angles.'

'So it could be a house?'

'Some sort of building, yes. But we actually now think it's more likely be a tomb.'

'A tomb?'

Aware the others were listening to their conversation, and equally aware of his own lack of knowledge of all things archaeological, he motioned for her to move away from them and she did. In the shade of the olive grove she explained, 'It may be an abandoned house or anything but, given the size and shape appears to be limited, we don't think it is a palace.'

'That's good news.' Her mouth dropped. 'I mean, good for the hotel, not for you.'

She shook her head. 'No, we still hope we will find something. It seems too small to be a building but it could be some sort of hole. Such as a grave.'

'Wait, one minute you're looking for a palace or a temple, now you say it's a tomb.' He was about ready to call rubbish on this entire project. 'How do you know the stones are even ancient?'

'We don't, you're right. The stones may not even be very old,' she said.

He was right! 'Good.'

'It could just be a cellar, or a hole someone had once dug to hide valuables in the World Wars.'

'That's interesting,' he said, suddenly alert to another possibility: the find might turn out to be valuable or interesting without being old enough to render the whole block of land protected.

'It would be, sure. But these stones—they seem older than that.'

His heart fell.

'Though it's just a hunch,' she added. Neither

was ready to admit winning, just as neither was ready to admit defeat.

She placed her hands in her pockets and shifted from foot to foot. 'You came to ask me to dinner.'

'I did,' he confirmed.

'I'm actually going to Joe's with the team, but you're welcome to join us.'

He looked around at the tired red faces of the archaeologists. They would probably be an interesting bunch under any other circumstances. But right now listening to talk of Greek tombs and lost treasures was just about the last thing he felt like doing. Even if it meant being with Rose.

He shook his head. 'Have a good evening,' he said and turned.

It's not your fault he's upset.

It wasn't and Alessandro was going to have to get used to disappointment.

She was silent through dinner with the team, letting them talk and speculate around her, wanting to be drawn into their infectious excitement, yet also wanting to be cautious.

If you do find something significant on his land you are still going to have to deal with him. Your lives will be as closely connected as ever...

As she walked back to the hotel, she resolved to go and speak to him, though she had no idea what she would say beyond apologising for her clumsy and unwelcome invitation to dinner. But he wasn't in his office when she knocked. She sent him a brief message to say she hoped they could talk properly the next day.

Anastasia was sitting out in the courtyard, looking up at the stars. This woman had faced so much sadness, yet she seemed so content sitting here, catching the evening breeze, looking at the stars through the leaves of the over-hanging tree.

How could Rose get some of that contentment? How could she make peace with the world, and Alessandro in particular?

'Do you mind if I join you?' Rose asked.

Anastasia jolted upright, as if she'd actually been dozing all along.

'Yes, yes, my dear. Of course.' She looked around, as though looking for her grandson.

'I've come looking for him, but I don't know where he is.'

'Not in his office?'

'No.'

The older woman raised an eyebrow. 'Then you should sit and wait for him.'

Rose fell gratefully into a chair. Her limbs ached and her shoulders screamed. She hoped she wouldn't have to do too many more fourteen-hour days before they found something.

'Can I ask you a question?' Anastasia asked.

'Of course.'

'Why are you so focused on looking for something that you don't even know exists?'

Rose shrugged. 'I have to look. I want to know, one way or another. Don't we always look for things, never knowing if we may not find them?'

'That's true. But make sure you don't miss what you do have.'

'Ah, subtle,' Rose replied.

Anastasia feigned insult.

'I know that was your less than subtle way of telling me to work things out with Alessandro.'

'I would never do that. I simply want you to see what is in your present, without looking too much into the past.'

'There are so many lessons to learn from the past. In particular, we can learn from mistakes in the past so we don't make them again in our future.'

Anastasia sighed. 'Ah, well. Sometimes it doesn't matter how well we live our lives, whether we are good people or not. Fate has other plans for us.'

Ashamed, Rose looked down. This woman had known more tragedies than anyone deserved to: losing a husband, then a son gone before his time, then a grandson and granddaughter-in-law before their children even knew them.

But Rose was no stranger to misfortune. She had lost people too.

'I get comfort from the past,' Rose admitted quietly.

'Comfort?'

'Yes. From the stories. The myths. I know they

are not all real, but I find comfort in them. I know there are tragedies, but the stories are also about overcoming adversity, about bravery. I love the story of Odysseus because he came home. It took him twenty years, and no one believed it was him, but he came home to his still-faithful wife. I don't care if it's true, but I think it's wonderful.'

For years and years after her father had left she had dreamt that he was actually off fighting a war and then had been detained for long years on his journey home—detained by shipwrecks, storms and wars.

Of course, her father hadn't returned, but that hadn't stopped her dreaming.

Anastasia squeezed her knee and said, 'Oh, Engoní.'

Rose knew enough Greek to know that she had just called her 'granddaughter'.

'The lovely Miss Rose came looking for you last night.'

Yiayia pulled him up in the kitchen the next morning.

'She did?'

'Yes. Where did you disappear to anyway?'

He turned and poured a cup of coffee. 'Just out.'

He'd walked and walked. And, before he knew it, he'd reached Gaios. Paxos wasn't large, but still, it wasn't a journey he was in the habit of making. After his strange and awkward conversation with Rose he'd needed to be alone with his thoughts.

Yesterday had started off awkwardly with Rose in the cave. His attempts to protect her feelings had been interpreted as rejection. He'd wanted to hold her all night, as he had that afternoon... stroking her, adoring her, loving her...but she'd made it clear they shouldn't make love again.

He'd hardly slept all night. She was right about describing it as torture—holding her to keep her warm, but not being able to be with her, had been torture.

It had become progressively worse. First with Demetri calling every hour, leaving messages demanding the start date be confirmed. And then Rose's discovery of the stone slabs. So they thought they'd found something? They hadn't yet. And so what if they hadn't had dinner together last night? Maybe they would tonight. And why, when they had both agreed to keep things platonic, was he still desperate to spend time with her?

She'd come looking for him. His grandmother's news shook away the last of his doubts and fears. It would be okay.

'What did she say?'

'Not much, just that she was looking for you.'

If only he hadn't decided to go on such a long walk. If only he'd been home to meet her.

* * *

That afternoon, he walked back down to the dig, determined that no matter what he would stay on top of his emotions. Even so, his heart raced and his stomach felt light as he approached. When it came to Rose, staying on top of his emotions was always a challenge.

He spotted her large white hat immediately, his eyes drawn to her like a magnet. Then another movement caught his eye. Ana was standing a few metres to Rose's left, waving to him.

What?

'Ali!' she called. Rose pulled herself up, shielded her eyes from the sun and looked in his direction. The light feeling in his stomach turned to stone and dropped.

He made his way down as Ana rushed to him.

'Isn't this great?' she said breathlessly.

'What are you doing here?'

'Helping with the excavation.'

Rose appeared behind Ana, brushing her hands off on her trousers.

'This was your idea?' he asked her.

'No! It was mine,' Ana said. 'I've been asking her for ages and she finally said yes.'

'Can I talk to you for a minute?' he muttered under his breath.

Ana stepped forward.

'No, not you, I want to speak with Rose.'

Ana rolled her eyes heavenward. A look passed

between Rose and his niece, followed by a slight nod from Rose. Ana turned back to the dig and Rose followed him to the tent.

'What's going on?' he said once they were out of earshot of the others.

'Just like she told you, she's been asking me for ages and I said yes. We always need extra hands to dig, carry…'

'Digging? Carrying? You should have asked me. What if she gets hurt?'

'She's not going to get hurt, it's perfectly safe. There's no need to go into over-protective mode.'

Maybe it was just the sun or the heat but his vision blurred. 'Are you suggesting she isn't my responsibility?'

Rose pulled a face he couldn't read.

'Because, for all intents and purposes, I'm her father.'

'I know that.' She touched his arm, but instead of the tingly pleasure he'd felt the other day now her hand was heavy. 'I know you raised her, I know how much you love and care about her. I'm saying she's sixteen and it is perfectly safe for her to be removing dirt from a dig.'

'She's a child.'

'And also a young adult. No one's asking her to push wheelbarrows or carry buckets of rocks.'

'That's beside the point.'

'Hang on, Alessandro, what exactly are you upset about?'

Rose was perfectly right. Ana wasn't doing anything dangerous. She was doing something she actually loved. And this, he hated to admit, was rare. Helping a team of excavators was definitely a better use of her time than looking at goodness knew what on her phone.

'You still should have asked me.'

'Fine, okay. Maybe we should have asked you. But, Alessandro, she's sixteen—she's going to be doing a lot of things without needing your permission soon.'

He was about to storm out of the tent when Rose grabbed a cold bottle of water from a nearby cool box and handed it to him. He wanted to push her hand away but thought better of it. Rose was right—launching into over-protective mode at this point was going to be completely unproductive. He snapped open the water and drank.

She pointed to a camp chair and he sat. She sat next to him. 'And, since we're talking about it, you should probably know that Lucas and a couple of his friends have expressed an interest in helping too.'

This was the limit. After everything he was doing for these kids, everything he had done...

'Don't you have enough people here?'

'Oh, wait, hang on! This isn't about protecting them at all. You just don't want extra bodies here, extra helpers. Oh, this is all about not wanting me to find anything.' She stood and placed her face in her hands.

'What? No.'

'So you want me to find something?'

'Well, I mean, if things were different of course I'd be delighted for you to dig up the Ark. But…'

'But things aren't different.' She finished his sentence. 'This is where we find ourselves. Here, on this piece of land.'

He shrugged. It was all he could do. They were stuck.

You can't go forward, but you can't go back.

'Ana's genuinely interested.'

He knew that. This was the first thing that had got her enthused in months.

'I'm happy for her to be interested. And, despite how it looks, I am trying to protect them. This hotel was meant to be their future. This is what their father wanted for them. I'm only trying to do what he would have wanted.'

She looked to the dig and sighed, giving him a moment to steal a glance at her. Her skin was flushed in the heat but not burnt. Her hair was tied back but messy. Small drops of sweat glistened on her collar bone and he fought the urge to kiss them away.

She turned back and said, 'But what about you, Alessandro? What do you want?'

You, he wanted to say.

You, forever.

But what would have been the point?

Rose was the only woman he wanted, the only women he'd ever wanted. His heart's deepest desire. She made everything else fade into the distance.

Except he couldn't let her. Duty, family, loyalty... he had to protect those things too. Because, if he didn't look after the kids, if he didn't do his duty to his family, then how could he ever offer himself to Rose?

He loved her. He'd always loved her and, he realised now that everything was hopeless, he always would.

The weather changed. It was Greece, so it was still hot, but something happened as September became October. The sting came out of the sun, it took slightly longer for the earth to warm each day and the air was faster to cool. Rose's skin was relieved but her heart was not. October meant the end of her time was coming. With each day she expected a call from the museum. In one week, the six weeks she'd told Alessandro she would need would be up.

The entire team was there that morning, as well as Ana, carrying each bucket to be carefully labelled. They had uncovered the extent of the two stone slabs and were now carefully digging trenches either side. The deeper they got, the closer they were to finding something. Or finding nothing at all.

Late morning, Lucas arrived. Not to help with the digging, but bringing cold water and snacks for the team.

'Does your uncle know you're here?' Rose asked.

Lucas grinned and shrugged. It was the same cheeky expression Alessandro sometimes gave her and Rose didn't know whether to feel happy or sad. His father, Theo, had probably been a lot like Alessandro.

Rose sat with Ana, having a break while she drank and ate.

'Everyone's quiet today.'

Rose agreed. 'It's make or break time. We're going home next week.'

'Even you?' Ana looked crestfallen.

There were no guarantees of anything. 'Probably even me.' It might not be next week but, no matter what happened, Rose would eventually leave.

'But if you find something you'll stay, won't you?' Ana asked.

'Oh, I...for a while, I guess.' Strangely, Rose hadn't spent much time considering what would happen if she did find something.

You don't believe you will, do you?

It wasn't that, she told herself. It was partly so as not to tempt fate, partly because so much depended on what it was they did find. And how upset Alessandro would be…

'But won't there be years of work to do?' Ana asked.

'Maybe, yes, but…'

'You don't actually believe you will find something, do you?' Ana looked at her, her face asking the question Rose had silently asked herself. The teenager was wise beyond her years.

'Of course, there are just lots of variables. If it's something amazing, of course I'll stay a bit longer.'

'Then I hope you find something amazing.'

Rose laughed, 'Thank you, that's nice.'

'And I think Ali would be happy if you stayed.'

'Oh, no, I don't think he'd be happy at all.'

'He'll get over the hotel thing.' Ana waved her hand as though the hotel, Alessandro's duty to his family, was merely a fly to be swatted away.

'I'm not sure he will. He's looking after your future. This hotel is meant for you and Lucas.'

'But we don't want it,' Ana whispered.

'But it's your legacy, your inheritance. It's what your father wanted.'

Rose could practically see the weight on Ana's shoulders as she replied, 'I want to be free, like you.'

Rose laughed. Because she wasn't free. Not really…because leaving here would be the hardest goodbye she'd ever had to make. Her heart was heavy. The rest of the world held no appeal, no excitement. This land, this place, was where she had felt more at home than, well, anywhere.

'Alessandro isn't about to go anywhere. Besides, it seems like Lucas is preparing to take over the hotels, and you're probably going to be able to do anything you want. In building this hotel, he's wanting to give you give you both a family legacy. I don't think he's honestly trying to tell you how to run your life.'

Rose hoped she wasn't wrong about this, for Ana's sake.

'He believes in duty,' Ana said. 'He goes on and on about it.'

'But I think he's mostly referring to his own, not yours.'

She saw the thoughtful look on Ana's face and stood. She had to get back to work.

'And if something happens to Lucas?' Ana asked.

'Nothing's going to happen to him,' Rose said without thinking. She sat back down with Ana and squeezed her arm. Life had taught this young woman to take nothing for granted. 'Seriously, it'll be okay. Alessandro isn't going anywhere for another fifty years, at which point Lucas will be running the business and you'll be happily working in a museum somewhere else in the world. You can make your own decisions. And if he tries to stop you, you tell me. Okay?'

Ana smiled and nodded. 'Okay.'

Rose stood again.

'Do you want kids?' Ana asked and her question hit Rose in the chest. If ever an adult was presumptuous enough to ask her that question, Rose usually declared loudly and strongly that, no, she did not.

She'd usually leave it at that, unless the presumptuous adult challenged her with a remark about how not wanting children was selfish.

'Selfish is having a kid and then abandoning them,' she would reply.

But this was not the answer for a teenager who could not remember her parents, whose parents had left because of tragedy and bad driving, not deliberate choice. It was not the answer for Ana, who was wide-eyed and simply curious, just wanting to know about Rose. And it was not the answer for Ana because, if Rose had ever been lucky enough to have a daughter like her, she knew she could never have left her.

'I don't know,' Rose replied honestly.

Ana stood and walked back to her buckets, seemingly satisfied by Rose's ambiguous answer.

Rose walked slowly back to her position, grateful Ana hadn't asked more. Because Rose wouldn't have known how to answer. All her life she'd been so sure that the answer to that question was a firm no. Rose intended to work all over the world; she intended to have a base, but not a home. A place where she would keep her books, out of season clothes and an address for her passport. And you didn't bring a child into the world to give them a base rather than a home.

But if she had a home?

Then the answer might be different.

You don't have a home, so keep digging!

And if a daughter happened to come into her life…a daughter like Ana? Then that might also be different.

Rose was crouched with Gabriel on the inside of the corner made by the slabs, sweeping the soil away carefully, when Gabriel cried out. Rose turned, looked over her shoulder and saw it.

A flash of green.

Bronze!

CHAPTER TWELVE

HER HANDS SHOOK as she held the three-thousand-year-old pendant.

It was burnished, but definitely gold. Maybe part of Odysseus' treasure. The link to Homer's hero was uncertain but the age, the significance, was not.

Ten years of work, fifteen years of study, twenty-five years of dreaming about it. And here it was—the discovery of a lifetime.

It was now after sunset and a small crowd was gathering. The atmosphere around the site was charged. They all watched her turn the gold pendant over in her hands.

A few hours after the tip of what had appeared to be a bronze sheet was revealed, the colour of the ground beneath her had changed from brown to gold and there it was: a pendant, intricately engraved with the figure of a griffin.

The bronze appeared to be a sheet and had possibly once covered what lay beneath. At some point, it had cracked and fallen in on what it covered. At that point, while they understood they had found something, the extent of it was unclear.

But the pendant sealed it. They had found treasure. A treasure that had either been hidden on purpose—perhaps to evade an invading army— or, more likely, given the structure and shape of the hole they were digging, from a grave, a tomb. They would need further investigation to know for sure what it was and how long it had been there.

Gabriel held out a plastic bag and Rose reluctantly placed the pendant in it.

She picked up her brush. 'You're still working?' Ana asked.

It hadn't occurred to Rose to stop yet. But perhaps she should. Now they had found gold, the site needed to be secured. They needed to inform the museum. Rose stood and brushed herself off.

'Ana, please don't tell anyone. Least of all your uncle. Not yet. Not until we know more and I've had a chance to call the museum.'

'Um…' Gabriel said. 'I think it's too late for that.'

Rose looked up the hill and saw Alessandro's imposing silhouette coming into view.

They'd found something. Bronze, Lucas had said as he'd passed his office. And then, as if it was being whispered on the breeze from the dig to his office, gold. Gold… Gold?

There were half a dozen people standing around the trenches by the stone slabs. The air buzzed with excitement. He found Rose in the crowd and met her eyes. Her mouth was clearly fighting back a smile, but her brown eyes sparkled.

Don't deny her this. She's excited and she's allowed to be.

'Can we talk?' she asked.

He nodded.

She followed him to where they couldn't be heard by the others aware that, even so, all eyes and ears were on them.

'Rumour has it you've struck gold.'

She nodded. She was trying so hard not to smile. She was probably wanting to jump up and down, but she was being calm. For him.

'We came across a bronze sheet or plate; it's hard to say just yet. But as we brushed the soil away we unearthed a gold pendant. It's beautiful. Engraved with a griffin. It could be a treasure hidden from invaders or robbers. Or it could be from a grave.'

A grave—Odysseus' grave. That was exactly what she'd hoped to find.

'So, what does it mean?'

'We don't know everything. We'll need to do some more precise dating but we are fairly confident that it's at least a thousand years old. Probably more.'

Alessandro knew that any artefacts older than five hundred years were deemed to be the property of the state. The Ministry of Culture would definitely issue a protection order over the site.

He sighed. 'I'm happy for you, I really am.'

'I know you are.' She was watching him for signs of anger, but he wasn't yet sure how he felt. He glanced back down at the dig. At Ana and Lucas talking excitedly with the team, Ana rocking back and forth on her heels. The pleasure of the kids was obvious, even from this distance. Next to him, Rose was vibrating; this was the most exciting moment of her career. No matter how disappointed he was personally, the find had made a lot of people happy. He swallowed hard.

'There are practicalities to discuss,' Rose said.

Were there ever. He had to cancel the builders and tell the bank.

'But first thing is, we can't tell anyone,' she said.

'What? I have to tell people and right away. I have to cancel the builders as soon as possible. Every day I don't, it's costing us thousands of euros.'

'If they find out that we've found something like this, the scavengers will come.'

'Scavengers? Are you suggesting we're all scavengers?'

'Not the Paxiotes, but word spreads. We've already found one gold pendant and there's every reason to believe there might be more. Even if there isn't, they will want to find something, and could destroy the entire site looking for it.'

'So what do you suggest I do? No, Rose, I can't put it off. I've already inconvenienced the builders enough.'

'Please, Alessandro. A day or two.' She pressed her palm to his arm. He froze and looked at it. It was covered in dust but he still wanted to pick it up and kiss it.

It felt as though they could never agree, that they were always at odds. Always travelling in opposite directions and trying to pull the rest of the world with them.

'Can you wait until tomorrow or the next day to tell the builders and the bank? I can make some phone calls and get some security.'

'Security guards?'

'Alessandro, there's gold. And goodness knows what else.' She squeezed his arm softly. If only he could give her everything she wanted, he'd happily give her the world.

It was already the evening and there was no point calling anyone now. Besides, there were quite a few people gathered.

'Are these all your people?' he asked.

She squinted and shook her head.

'Then it seems that word's already got out,' he said. 'What will you do?'

'I'll have to stay here. Keep watch.'

'All night? By yourself?'

'Gabriel will stay with me.'

Her second-in-command, the eager Frenchman.

'No, I'll stay with you.'

'Alessandro, you don't have to.'

If Rose was going to sit outside all night protecting a buried treasure, he was going to be with her.

'It's my land, my responsibility. I'll keep watch.'

CHAPTER THIRTEEN

THANK GOODNESS IT was a still, dry night.

In the end, they organised shifts. Gabriel and another team member took the first, while Rose and Alessandro ate and tried to sleep. At midnight, predictably just as she'd finally drifted off to sleep, Alessandro woke her with a gentle knock on her door.

Sitting outside alone in the moonlight with Alessandro was probably not the wisest thing for her to do at this point in time. He was keeping his disappointment to himself, but it was clearly written across his beautiful features. She wanted to reach over, rub his arm, hug him, but sensed her touch would be as unwelcome as the gold pendant she'd dug up that afternoon.

On the plus side, he did have a flask of hot, strong coffee.

They sat on camp chairs, watching over the darkness of the site, and sipped in silence until their cups were empty and the silence uncomfortable.

'Thank you again for sitting out here with me,' she said.

'Of course. I don't want someone coming and looting the place any more than you do.'

She wrapped her arms around herself. 'It's good of you. I know this isn't easy for you and I appreciate it.'

'Here, I've got some blankets.' He riffled through the bag at his feet and handed her a blanket.

'Always the boy scout,' she said, pulling it around herself, trying not to remember the night in the cave, the fire or holding him...loving him.

He grinned and shrugged, as he did, giving her a flash of the young Alessandro.

It reminded her of her encounter with Lucas today, the Andino shrug and grin: cheeky; light-hearted. Alessandro used to do it all the time in Athens...not so much now. It was a family gesture. Theo had probably done it too. Theo, who always seemed to come between them.

'Tell me about Theo,' she said.

'Haven't I already?'

'Not directly. You talk about him but you never told me about how you feel about him.'

He sighed deeply, soulfully. 'I don't know. He was my big brother. And he was so good at everything. Lots of people hate their older siblings, but I adored him and worshiped him.'

'How much older was he?'

'Eight years older, but it seemed so much more.

He threw himself into the business when he was only a teenager and he'd accomplished so much before he was even thirty. Almost like he knew he didn't have eighty years to live.'

Rose wasn't quite sure what to say. It seemed even more of a tragedy that Theo had died so young and yet had packed so much into his short life: professional success, finding true love and having two beautiful children. 'Anyway, I wanted to be just like him, but I wasn't.'

Rose laughed. 'What do you mean?'

'He was good at sports and sailing.'

'And so are you!'

'He was great at running the business.'

'And so are you. It's gone from strength to strength since you've been running it.'

'Who told you that? Google?'

'Yes, but also everyone here—your grand-mother, Ana and Lucas, anyone in Ninos who has spoken about you. Why? Don't you believe it?'

'Because he was so much better at everything. He was a natural. And he understood about family and loyalty without having to go through tragedy to see it,' he said.

'I think you're being way too hard on yourself.' She turned to him and, in the moonlight, saw him resting his forehead on his hands.

'I've tried my best, but father always let me know that I needed to do better. That I should be more like Theo. I didn't even think of going into the family business because he had it all so amazingly under control.'

'Hang on, did you study journalism and politics because you wanted to or because your father made you feel that you weren't good enough to do this?' She spread her arms out at the land before them.

'Maybe a bit of both. If he were still alive, then who knows what he would have done?'

'And who knows what he wouldn't have?'

She couldn't believe he was comparing himself to his late brother and coming up short. 'Alessandro, you're amazing. Theo would be so proud. Proud of the way you've run the business. But, most of all, he'd be so proud and grateful for the way you've raised his children. And you have proven your father completely wrong. You're allowed to think of what you want.'

The only indication he gave that he'd heard her was the quiet hum coming from his direction.

'Even now, even with me ruining your plans, even now they'd been proud. They'd be proud of the hospitality and equanimity you've shown me. They'd be proud of the way you protected me from the storm when we were on the island.'

Now he turned and looked but still didn't speak. She wanted to get through to him, but it was as if her words were bouncing off him.

This hotel was the family's plan. It was the one thing Alessandro couldn't give them. It had never been just about the money, it had always been about his family's wishes. And the fact that, no matter what he did, Alessandro would still feel as though he didn't measure up to his brother. Which was ridiculous. Alessandro was the most loyal, hard working, loving man she'd ever known.

'You are enough,' she said.

He didn't respond but she thought she saw him shake his head.

They didn't speak for the next while. He looked down at his phone and Rose ruminated on the conversation they'd just had. She watched the moon rise higher, felt the air get ever so slightly cooler. When she stood and stretched, the spell broke and he finally spoke.

'I did get a call from the builders. They'd heard.'

'About the gold?'

He nodded. 'Good news travels fast.'

'What did you tell them?'

'Like you asked, I didn't confirm anything. You were right about needing security.'

Rose knew she wouldn't like what she was about to hear.

'He offered to come down with his excavator in the middle of the night and clear the whole place out.'

'What? Are you serious?'

He grimaced. 'I told him not to even think

about it. That we had the world's toughest security guards watching the place.'

She giggled; neither of them could ever be called the 'world's toughest'.

'Thank you. That was good of you.'

'Of course I told him to back off—you don't think I would have agreed with him?'

'No, no, but I do know that this is hard for you. I do know this isn't what you wanted.'

He hunched over in his chair and rubbed his hands. She reached over and rubbed his back. His shoulders were solid and warm. She wanted to wrap her arms around him completely. To reassure him. To love him.

He turned his head and the smile on his soft lips made her insides flip.

'You could try and get a little sleep. You've got another big day ahead tomorrow,' he said.

'What about you?'

'I'll watch.'

'Don't steal the treasure.' She yawned.

He laughed.

'I won't. I'll guard it with my life.' She shivered. And not from the cold but from the desire, the want, brewing inside her.

How could she still want to kiss him when he must despise her? Nothing made sense.

Because, ironically, now that she might be staying on Paxos for a longer stay, she and Alessandro really couldn't be together. The treatment he was giving her this evening was the coolest since she'd arrived on the island, cooler even than the first day when he'd tried to convince her to leave.

With his head bowed, she could study him unconstrained. If only she could hug those shoulders which were carrying too much unnecessary weight. If only she could touch his skin, feel his hands on her body again.

It was strange that, now that any chance of them working through their differences had evaporated completely, she could actually imagine herself staying. It was perverse.

It was the strangest feeling, wanting to stay here. Ana had been right—this find was too big to walk away from. She wanted to see what else they found. She wanted to analyse each piece, study them, see them safely to a museum. There were months, maybe years, of work to be done here.

And there was Alessandro.

Of course you want to stay. You want to be with him. He's the best man you've ever known. The best man you'll ever know.

Yesterday, the thought of finding something wonderful had been so appealing. But now? Now it was real and not just a dream, it was far more complicated then she'd realised. There were so many things to think about.

She couldn't leave Paxos immediately; she had to see this through to the end and find out what else was in this pit or grave. It would take months at least. She was staying for a while, but now she needed her space from Alessandro to guard her heart as much as ever.

It was all such a mess. A list of things to do assembled in her head: she had to let her work know; she had to talk to the museum in Athens about personnel, logistics, money.

She couldn't keep staying at his hotel all this time, could she? It wasn't part of their original deal. It certainly wasn't part of her original plan. She seriously doubted Alessandro wanted her around now that she had destroyed his plans to extend the hotel.

Besides, it was better that she left first. It was always better to leave first.

She stood. Moving away from his gaze was for the best. She began to pace.

'What's wrong? They won't come with the excavators. I told them not to and I'm pretty sure he was just trying me out.'

'It's not that.'

'Then what?'

'I think I should move out.'

'Leave the hotel?' he asked.

'I can't stay now, Alessandro. Not when I ruined everything for you.'

He stood as well. 'I don't blame you for this. It isn't your fault. Well, it is your discovery, but I don't blame you. It's just circumstance.'

He lifted his hand, as though to touch her, but dropped it just before their bodies made contact.

He knew as well as she did the sparks that would fly through them if they did.

'I feel like I would be taking advantage, and it wouldn't be fair.'

'But it's also about me, isn't it?'

She had to be honest, there was no point being otherwise. 'Alessandro, you know I love being with you, and that's exactly why I have to leave. We can't keep doing this to one another.'

I don't think I could get over you again.

'I really don't mind you staying.' He didn't look at her as he spoke but kicked the ground.

'But I mind. It wouldn't be fair.'

'On you or me?'

'On both of us.' She swallowed hard, wishing she'd had the foresight to have this conversation closer to dawn, when at least one of them could leave. Now they were stuck sitting here with one another for the next five hours. *Awkward much?*

'Okay,' he said and nodded. 'I understand, and you're probably right.'

Even though he had agreed, her heart fell. It was what she wanted, wasn't it? Then why did she feel so awful?

She paced around the site for a while, more to keep awake than to keep watch. When her legs began to ache, she sat down again next to Alessandro, who was still hunched over his phone. She must've dozed off for a while, when a noise in the bushes startled them both at one point, but it turned out just to be a goat.

'I hope it's okay,' she said and she thought she saw a sad smile on his face. They settled back down. It certainly wasn't Demetri and his bull-dozer.

Eventually, the sky lightened from black to blue to pink. Her team began to return even before the sun was actually above the horizon, and at that point Alessandro took his leave.

His limbs were heavy when he walked into the kitchen. Ana was poring over three books open on the table in front of her and Yiayia was making coffee.

'Did you know that they actually don't know where Odysseus died?'

He shook his head. Homer and Odysseus were not his favourite people this morning.

Lucas was typing something on his laptop. 'Everyone's talking about this,' he said. 'It's the most exciting thing to happen on Paxos since the Nazis invaded.'

'Oh, Lucas, really,' Yiayia chided.

'Good morning, *kamari mou*, are you going to try and get some sleep?' she asked Alessandro.

He shook his head. 'I've got things to do. Lucas, who is *everyone*? Who knows about Rose's discovery?'

Lucas shrugged. 'Everyone around here. Kids at school.'

So maybe not everyone. The find was certainly exciting for the locals but probably wasn't the first thing on the international news. It was one more thing to look into today. One more thing to deal with.

'Oh, Yiayia, Rose will be moving out of the flat.'

'And moving in with you?' Ana asked, wide-eyed.

'What? No! Ana, how could…?'

He regretted his tone and her face fell.

'No, she's probably moving back to Myra's.'

'Didn't you tell her not to leave?' Ana's eyes, which had been so wide and bright moments ago, now clouded over.

You did that.

'She doesn't want to stay in the flat.'

'Why not? What's wrong with it?'

Its proximity to me, he thought.

'What happened between you?' Ana probed. She was too smart, this one.

'Nothing.'

Not nothing. Something. Everything. But nothing any more.

'Now that she'll be staying a little longer, she doesn't think it would be appropriate to take advantage of my hospitality.'

'I don't understand. Now, more than ever, she should be staying. With you.'

'Shh, Ana,' her great-grandmother admonished.

'I see the way you look at her.' Ana had no intention of heading Yiayia's warning.

He shook his head.

'I know you like her.'

'We're friends,' he said. It was such a loaded word—friends. Were they even friends? In between 'acquaintance' and 'lover' came 'friend', but were they even that?

'I love her!' Ana cried.

'You can't love her—you hardly know her.'

'I love her and I want to be just like her.'

He grimaced. This was not how it had been meant to go. Ana was not meant to become attached to Rose. She was not meant to be upset by her departure.

Just as he wasn't. The whole point of not sleeping together again had been to protect his heart. But that ship had sailed already. That ship had sailed almost a decade and a half ago.

'Don't mind her,' Yiayia said. 'She's young and doesn't understand how complicated real life is.'

Lucas watched on as the scene played out but Ana, standing now, was not going to stop. 'I do understand. I understand that you resent her because you can't build Papa's hotel. But that was Papa's dream, not mine, not Lucas's and I don't think it's yours. I think your dream…'

Yiayia held up a hand in front of her. 'Shh,

now, Ana, please stop. Please let your uncle and I talk. Go and get dressed.'

Alessandro's heart pounded but his skin felt cold. Ana, for all her precocity, had never spoken to him so bluntly. He wasn't angry, just stunned.

'She's not leaving, she's going back to Myra's. You can still see her.'

She just doesn't want to see me. I've been a fool. I've tried to stop something that couldn't be stopped.

Our fates were sealed three thousand years ago.

Ana looked at him for a long while, but still didn't leave. He didn't have the strength to tell her to leave, waiting for her next onslaught of teenaged wisdom.

'They were our parents, but we don't remember them. You're the only parent we remember,' Lucas said.

'I know,' Alessandro said.

'And we want you to be happy. It's not that we don't care about the hotel, but we care more about you.'

'The hotel is for you. It was your father's dream. It's what we all want.'

Ana and Lucas exchanged glances. Not for the first time he felt ganged up on by a pair of kids.

'We do want the hotel, but not at all costs. Don't you see?' Ana asked.

See? He saw two confused and upset teens.

One day, when the excitement of Rose's find wore off, they would regret not having their father's legacy on the island. They would regret that Paxos hadn't got the development it so desperately needed. They were too young to see it now, but one day this discovery would be in the past and what about their future?

'I'm sorry that Rose is moving out, but it is for the best.'

'Best for who?'

This time it wasn't one of the twins asking.

It was his grandmother.

CHAPTER FOURTEEN

ROSE'S DAY PASSED in a sleep-deprived blur, but eventually the adrenaline and caffeine kicked in. The team was delighted to unearth more treasures—two silver cups. The mood was buoyant. This really was turning out to be the once-in-a-lifetime find she had dreamed of.

She'd also managed to get in contact with the museum, and two security guards from the Ministry of Culture arrived late afternoon. By the time she dragged herself up the hill to the hotel that afternoon, she was ready to sleep for a week.

But she couldn't. She had one more thing to do first.

Myra was happy to have Rose back and could offer her a room of her own now that the summer peak had passed. The museum was also more than happy to pay whatever it was going to take to discover the full extent of their dig. Things were looking up.

Rose returned to the hotel that evening to gather her things. She wanted to get out of there, get back to Myra's before she accidentally ran into him again. She could just leave without saying goodbye.

But she couldn't leave without saying goodbye to Ana, Lucas or Anastasia; that would be unforgivable. She had to risk seeing Alessandro again, hope that he too was going to keep his distance from her. It was hard knowing he was out in the world, seeing him but not with her, but not being able to hold him was the hardest of all.

Once she had packed, she wheeled her case to the kitchen door and knocked.

Ana bounded out. 'What did you find today? I'm so bummed it was a school day.' Then she spied the suitcase. 'You're really going? But Alessandro...'

Anastasia touched Ana's arm and she stopped speaking.

'I came to say goodbye.'

'You don't have to go,' Ana said.

'I do.'

'Why? It's much nicer here. And closer.'

Ana made a good point. But it was done.

'It's not right for me to stay.'

'Did my stupid uncle say something stupid?'

Rose smiled at Ana's vehemence. 'No, he didn't do or say anything. But I can't keep relying on his hospitality.'

'Then it must be because of us.' Lucas frowned.

Rose's heart broke at that moment.

'No. Not at all. I've loved staying with you, and you can come and say hello any time. I'll be at the dig. Or at Myra's. I'm not going far.'

They looked at her as though they didn't believe her.

'It isn't about you,' she assured them, as much for herself as the kids.

'Let her go, *agapi mou*,' she said.

The twins gave Rose one last, sad glance then walked inside.

'You understand, don't you?' Rose asked Anastasia.

'I understand. I don't agree, but I do understand.'

Rose hugged her and turned to leave before she burst into tears.

Rose stood at the road and waited for the car to drive her to the village.

Then it must be because of us.

The look on their face had been heart-breaking—and heart-broken. She would have stayed for the twins, were it not for their uncle.

No, she couldn't stay for them, because it wasn't right. It wouldn't be right to take advantage of Alessandro's hospitality now that she was stopping the extension. Putting a halt to his brother's dreams.

And it wouldn't be right for either of them to be so close together, spending so much time with one another. That would be the most unfair of all.

Was this what her father had felt? Had he, in fact, just been too gutless to say goodbye?

Saying goodbye to the twins hurt her physically, and they were not her own; she had only known them for a matter of weeks.

She wasn't leaving the twins, but she was most definitely leaving their uncle. Though it was going to hurt to see them. It was going to hurt to hear them talk about him while not being a real part of their lives.

Her thoughts circled back. Was this how her father had felt—that he couldn't stay in contact with Rose because it would hurt too much?

She shook her head. She still didn't forgive him; a better man would have overcome that fear.

But perhaps now she did finally understand that a reason for his absence might have been that he'd actually loved her.

CHAPTER FIFTEEN

THERE WAS A lot to do—people to call, plans to remake—but this time he wasn't going to make the mistake of fourteen years ago. This time he was going to talk to Rose before he made too many other plans.

His eyes were drawn, as usual, straight to her white hat. She was standing with Gabriel and a woman, hunched over an object she was holding in both hands.

More treasure.

But this time his heart didn't drop. It sang. The find was probably turning out to be bigger than Rose had even hoped. He waved and caught Gabriel's eye. Gabriel nudged Rose and she looked in his direction. He noticed her shoulders drop. She passed the object to Gabriel and walked slowly over to Alessandro, each footstep heavy with reluctance.

She took her hat off and wiped her brow with her long sleeve as she reached him. Her face was pink, flushed and healthy, though some dark circles were under her eyes. Neither of them had got much sleep in the past few days.

'How's the dig going?' he asked.

'We don't have to talk about this, you know.'

'I know, but I want to,' he said honestly. 'I want to hear all about it.'

'Alessandro…' She sighed. 'There's no need to be polite. I know this has hurt you.'

There was genuine pain in her eyes. The greatest moment of her career had been tarnished by him and he hated it.

But fortunately it was within his power to fix it.

The idea had been percolating since the night they had watched over the site. At first, he'd thought her timing couldn't be worse, telling him she wanted to move out of the hotel while they'd still had five hours to sit alone with one another.

But it had been sitting there in silence next to her in the moonlight, looking over the site and wondering what lay beneath the surface, that the idea had come to him. He'd done some research via that great oracle, the Internet.

But the conversation he'd had with his family had sealed it—they loved him regardless of whether he could fulfil Theo's wishes. They'd assured him that this was what they wanted, that there would always be a chance for another hotel but never a chance for this.

He had their full and enthusiastic support—

especially Ana's, who'd had to be told many times that it was just an idea and not to announce it to the world.

He still had many, many people to speak to—the builders, architects and the government. There were approvals and all sorts of things. It wasn't going to happen straight away, but that was also okay. Good things, important things, didn't need to be rushed.

Not when he was so sure.

As he was now.

'I'm going to build a museum.' He could feel the tremor in his voice. He was going to build a museum—not a hotel, but a museum! He loved the way that sounded.

'I'm going to build a museum to showcase what you find. To show the history of Paxos and the Ionian Sea.'

She looked at him as though he was mad. He felt a bit crazy, not exactly like himself, and yet more like himself than he'd felt in years.

'I haven't figured out all the details yet, and there's obviously a lot to sort out, but I wanted you to know that that's what I'm going to do.'

He waited, knowing the grin on his face looked foolish and not caring. Rose's jaw dropped and her face seemed redder.

Her voice was soft. 'But I don't understand how. You can't just build something here, even if it is a museum. We're still digging. We're going to have to survey the whole area.' She closed her eyes and drew in a deep breath. Finally, she reached over and touched his elbow. 'It's a lovely, lovely thought, but I don't see how it could work.'

Luckily, he was several steps ahead of her and he just smiled. 'Yes, I've thought of all that. See that land over there?' He pointed at the hill and across the road to the same block of land he'd once told her was unsuitable for the hotel. It wasn't large enough for the hotel, and didn't have the ocean view, but for the early stages of the museum, it was perfect. 'Assuming a survey doesn't find anything there, the government will agree to lease it to us. The building could start as soon as the survey is done.'

She shook her head. 'They take time to plan; you can't just build one.'

'This wouldn't be the completed museum. It would just be the beginning. It would be a place for you to store the things you find, a place if you want to have offices. I think we could design that reasonably quickly. I've been in touch with an architect friend—'

'You've—you've spoken to an architect?' she spluttered.

'I've spoken to a few people, just to see what can be achieved. But I haven't made any decisions. I wanted to know if it was even possible before I spoke with you.'

Her mouth fell. 'You're really serious.'

'I'm very serious,' he said. 'I've never been more serious about anything in my life.' He picked up her hand. It was trembling. Or maybe that was his.

'Why?' she asked. Her voice was small, but her eyes were big.

'Because I've been too focused on one thing for too long. I've been worried so much about Theo's dreams for the children's future that I didn't think of their own wishes. I thought I was doing the best by them by doing what their father wanted, but the best thing for them is what they want, what they're interested in.'

Rose bit her lip and turned round to look back at her colleagues and the dig. 'I never met Theo or his wife but, given that he was your brother, I think he must've been a very good man. And I think that, if Theo and Arianna had known about this, he wouldn't want to be building a hotel here.'

His heart swelled. A very good man? That was what she'd called him. A very good man...but was that going be enough?

'It's funny, the kids told me the same thing when I suggested the plan to them.'

She turned back to face him, her golden eyes bright with excitement. 'You've talked to them too?'

'I asked them before I made any calls. I wanted to ask them before I came to you.'

She nodded. He wished he knew what she was thinking. He knew the plan had holes, he knew that a million things would have to go right to make this work, but he had to try.

'They adore you, you know.'

She kicked the ground. 'I adore them too.'

He looked into the distance, closed his eyes and drew a deep breath, but he needed courage more than air.

Now.

'Rose, there's something else.'

'Something else?'

'I want you to help me with the museum.'

'Help? How? I don't know anything about planning or building.'

'Run it, once it's built. Or whatever you like. I want you to stay.'

'Here?'

'Here with me. I've been a fool, not realising this all along. Your discovery is fantastic for the island. It will bring tourists in more than any hotel. I was hoping you would run the museum—after you've finished excavating, that is. I know it's not a major museum, but you'd be the director. You'd have total control. And you would be able to run the excavation for as long as it takes.'

'Oh.' She turned and looked at the dig as though the answer was there. He fought the urge to spin her back to him. *Me. The answer is behind you.* Why was she taking so long to answer? He was the one who had been so slow to figure this out.

'And if I don't stay?' she asked. 'What about the museum?'

'I'll do it anyway. But I want you to be the one to set it up.'

'Why?'

Tell her.

'I love you. I want you to stay with me.'

She was still, unnervingly so. Almost as though she hadn't heard. Finally, she turned. 'It's a lot to take in. I'd have to leave London. The university.'

'I know, I'd be asking a lot, but hopefully giving you a lot. Everything I can. No one else has ever come close to making me feel what I do when I'm with you.' Maybe all this time he'd been subconsciously waiting for her. 'I love you, Rose. I've always loved you and I want to be with you. I don't have any intention of ever letting you go again.'

She covered her face with her hands. Was she hiding her joy or her distress?

'I don't know,' she said.

'You don't know if you love me? Or you don't know if you will stay?'

'I need time, please. I need some time to think. To process this.'

Shouldn't she be able to answer a question like that right away?

You took weeks to figure this out.

Not just weeks—it had taken him well over a decade to realise that he didn't have to block out what he wanted in his life in order to do the right thing by his brother. He's been trying to be his brother, to replace him. And Theo wouldn't have expected or even wanted that. Alessandro hadn't had to sacrifice his own life entirely to do the right thing by the kids and he saw that now.

Rose had her own worries and he needed to respect that.

'I'm not going to leave you. Never. I'm never leaving Paxos for good, so I'll never be able to leave you.'

She half-sighed, half-grimaced.

'I just need time. This is…big. Can I sleep on it?'

Sleep? A whole day? Could he wait that long? He'd have to.

Rose turned and walked back down the hill, hardly feeling her feet. Was she floating? She certainly felt strange; her limbs tingled, her heart raced. He loved her. He wanted her to stay. He was building a *museum*. It was too much to process.

She reached the dig and looked down to the place where she'd been sitting prior to his arrival, but suddenly didn't know what to do. He'd just offered her his life and she had sent him away. She spun and looked back up the hill. Should she call him back? He'd disappeared from the horizon. Should she chase after him?

But if she did, what would she say? Could she stay? Could she be with him—for ever?

Her hands picked up a brush and she knelt, on automatic pilot.

'Did he come to try and persuade us to leave again?' Gabriel asked.

Rose shook her head. Thank heavens Gabriel didn't ask any more questions. She wasn't ready to tell them about the museum—they'd all be delighted. She'd lose all sense of rational thought.

Her heart was telling her—yelling at her—to race back up the hill to Alessandro and throw herself into his arms.

But that would be foolish, like walking off a cliff and straight into heartbreak.

If you walk off the cliff, he might catch you...

Could the museum really happen? Was it just a pie-in-the-sky plan?

No. She knew Alessandro better than that. He wasn't one for making fanciful plans that were easily abandoned. He saw things through. For the last six weeks he'd been trying to achieve the plans his dead brother had made years ago. No, Alessandro was not one to change course quickly, or on a whim. He believed in this museum.

And he believes in you.

She wanted to laugh and cry at the same time. Could she stay on Paxos, keep working on the site? That part of his question was easy—yes, she could. She'd love nothing more than to see this excavation through to the end.

It was the second part of the question that was the real problem. She kept working, the smooth, monotonous motion of brushing the dirt away soothing her body, and after a while her mind. *Sleep on it.* What was she thinking? How on earth was she possibly going to sleep while she was thinking about this?

She could stay on Paxos and be with Alessandro. Have the life they'd planned when she'd been twenty.

And a family.

Staying with him on Paxos would mean staying with the children. It would mean not letting them down, and that was another thing entirely.

She could never let Ana and Lucas down, she realised with a certainty that took her completely by surprise. She also knew with certainty that she'd never let Alessandro down either. His happiness was inextricably linked to hers. That had become so apparent over the last day, when her joy at the discovery had been tempered by his sadness.

No, her reservations were not about her feelings for the children.

'Oh, no. What am I doing?' she muttered and stood.

Gabriel looked up. 'What's wrong?'

'I'm an idiot, that's what's wrong.' She put down her brush. 'I've got to go.'

She was sweating, panting so hard she could hardly make herself heard when she called out to him. He kept getting further and further away.

She stopped, drew in some hard, deep breaths and yelled as loudly as she could, 'Alessandro!'

He stopped but didn't turn. Her heart plummeted.

She called again, 'Alessandro.'

This time he turned and moved slowly back down the hill to her. Was he upset? She couldn't tell; his face was expressionless, his step heavy.

She ran up the hill as fast as she could, and thankfully he met her halfway.

She tried to talk but her throat was dry and there was no air in her lungs.

'I've thought about it,' she gasped.

'That was quick.' He was uncertain, so she reached for his arm and squeezed it while she caught a few more breaths.

'I'm sorry it took me that long.' She couldn't hold back a smile. She was going to spend her life with Alessandro on Paxos.

He lifted his head and a smile began to grow on his lips.

She took the last step towards him and he threw his arms around her. She was home.

He held her close, still panting, his heart racing

against her cheek. Her gaze found his, but just for long enough for her to nod and let him know that her answer was yes. Then she closed her eyes and her lips met his. The kiss was sweet, tender and promising for ever.

When they pulled apart, he asked, 'Really? You will stay?'

'I will stay for ever. I love you, Alessandro.'

She felt the tension escape from his body in a rush.

'Oh, thank God. I just need to hear you say it.' He pulled her tighter and kissed her again.

But she wasn't done and pulled back.

'I love you, Alessandro Andino.'

'I love you too, Dr Rose Taylor.'

He squeezed her hand. 'Do you want to get back to work?'

She laughed. 'Not just yet. Whatever's buried there has waited thousands of years. It can wait a little longer.' She took his hand and led him back to the hotel.

EPILOGUE

It was a glorious Greek day. The sky was the colour of the flag and the sun bright, but a gentle spring breeze kept the air fresh. Rose was nervous but excited. The island was packed with visitors this weekend, but not the usual tourists but academics from the museum in Athens, Rose's colleagues from London—or, ex-colleagues now—and some representatives from the Ministry of Culture. They were all here for the opening of the small museum that had been built to showcase the Tomb of the Bronze Age Warrior.

The things they had found were even more remarkable then she'd ever let herself hope. Since the initial discovery, Rose and her team had uncovered bronze basins, weapons and armour. They had uncovered beads made of amethyst, amber and silver and more than thirty stone seals, intricately carved with images of goddesses, lions and bulls. This was one of the most remarkable finds made anywhere in Greece in the last decade.

Several months after they'd first found the

items, they'd finally reached the bottom and confirmed what they had suspected—a largely intact skeleton confirmed they had found a tomb. The scientific dating had confirmed Rose's greatest hopes—the tomb did, in fact, date back to the Bronze Age.

Even if she hadn't found Odysseus, she had found the final resting place of a Bronze Age warrior king.

The grave was three and a half thousand years old so did indeed date to the time of the battle of Troy and Odysseus' journey as told in Homer's stories.

The grave was now covered with an impressive roof, protecting the ruins from the elements, with a raised walkway allowing visitors to observe the archaeologists at work. The plan was now to carefully excavate the entire site. Even if they did not find another grave or remnant of buildings, simply analysing the area and the soil might give them further clues about Bronze Age life on Paxos.

They'd found over a thousand objects in all; it was going to take many years to preserve and curate all of them, as well as learning as much as one could from each of them. The objects were beautiful, but they could also tell so much about the past as well—the story of the man they were buried with, but also the story of the world in which he'd lived.

Today was a celebration; a large party had been planned at the hotel afterwards to welcome their visitors and thank the locals for their support.

Rose wore a long, flowing blue-and-white patterned dress, her red hair flowing in graceful waves around her shoulders. Spotting her at the entrance, Alessandro went to her and slipped his arm around her waist. 'I'm so proud of you.' He kissed her cheek.

'What for?' she asked.

'All of this,' he said, gesturing to the crowd around them.

'No.' She laughed. 'I did the easy stuff. You did this. I'm proud and so grateful you used your money and your time to create this.'

'I can't believe I ever wanted to do otherwise,' he replied.

'I can. You were only trying to build the future for this family that your brother had envisaged. And that's not a bad thing. He hadn't counted on any of this. I know, if he were still here, this is exactly what he would have done as well.'

Rose squeezed his arm and her heart flooded with joy. The past three years had been the most amazing of her life. The museum was a joint project between the Andino family and the National Museum. Some of the items would be on display in Athens, but many would remain on Paxos in the newly built museum.

It had been a busy couple of years on the island. In addition to the museum, they had built more accommodation nearby, long- and short-term stays, because the academics who came to study tended to want to stay for months at a time.

Alessandro sometimes said he found it hard to believe he could ever have objected to the excavation. The prestige and revenue it had brought to the business was remarkable, and beyond any of their expectations. However, the sheer joy and excitement that the discovery had brought to the village and his family was worth so much more.

Ana was obsessed with all things ancient Greek and was now at university in Athens. Lucas was interested in the hotel business, which he hoped to help grow and solidify, and he was intending to study business management in Athens.

Now that the twins were old enough that Alessandro and Rose could think about travelling and exploring the world together, the only place they wanted to be was on Paxos.

'You've made me happier than I've ever been,' she said to Alessandro, and he bent his head to kiss her. Softly at first, then deepening into something that sent ripples out to her toes.

A groan from a pair of teenagers reminded them where they were.

'Ah, leave them be, they deserve this day,' Yiayia said.

Alessandro was no longer just a hotel developer.

He was a benefactor, builder of a museum which, even though it was only just officially opening, was already acclaimed around the world. He had been invited to other museum openings, invited to speak at conferences about the way his family had handled the find and how he had worked with the local and national governments to design and build the museum on Paxos.

Somehow, at forty-one years of age, he'd found himself forging a new career, one that drove him with a new passion. He found himself thinking of returning to finish the university degree he'd abandoned, much to the feigned horror of Ana and Lucas. He reassured them all that any study he did would be remote; he had no intention of leaving Rose on Paxos. Or anywhere, for that matter.

Rose no longer mourned the lost years without Alessandro; what they had now was wonderful. The future was too bright to dwell too much on the past. She twisted the wedding ring on her finger, gold and simple. She spent too much time with her hands in dirt for anything too intricate. But to her it was more precious than any of the treasures she'd found in the grave.

Their wedding had been here, at the hotel overlooking the Ionian Sea. Her mother and friends from Britain had made the trip, but they were outnumbered by all the locals. Alessandro had invited almost everyone on Paxos. They had eaten and drunk all day and danced into the night.

And the bride had worn white.

* * * * *

If you enjoyed this story, check out these other great reads from Justine Lewis

Fiji Escape with Her Boss
Billionaire's Snowbound Marriage Reunion

Available now!